C000193595

## Praise for Paolo Maurensig

"Paolo Maurensig is an arresti... ........ .... ...g recent Italian writers."
*New York Times*

"In Paolo Maurensig, a new grand master of the novel has emerged."
*The Times*

●

## Praise for Game of the Gods

"Italian novelist Maurensig spins an intriguing historical narrative of Indian chess master Malik Mir Sultan Khan (1903–1966) … Maurensig's tragic tale of genius and destiny duly salvages a forgotten hero."
*Publishers Weekly*

"With his elegant writing, and via an intriguing chess game, Maurensig relates the life and deeds of an extraordinary character lost to history."
*Il Messaggero*

"Maurensig has not only given us another great character from the enchanting world of chess—in these pages we find the spirit of an entire era. This

novel has deep historical roots, numerous surprising twists, and contains infinite worlds in which karma provides many sharp turns to existence."
*Gli amanti dei libri*

"The passion for the game of chess in *Game of the Gods* is linked to themes of another order: the scenario of war, the element of racial distinctions and colonialism, the different conceptions of life in the East and the West. The elegance with which Maurensig manages to tie these into the plot is another of the typical elements of this author, and a merit of this book: a fluid novel that weaves historical reality and literary inventiveness in an astounding and fascinating way."
*Libri la mia vita*

"*Game of the Gods*, the fictional story of Sultan Khan, who truly was one of the strongest chess players of his time, is of such beauty that it leaves one astonished, even in the face of sadder and more painful events."
*L come Libro*

"Maurensig has the incredible gift of bringing back dreams that seemed to have vanished. Drawing fully from the great Kiplingian literature and reconverting it to the author's central European figure is not at all easy. But Maurensig is a writer

of immense value. This book is a jewel, a gift."
FABIO PONZANA, blogger

"The novel is a beautiful fresco of cultural clashes and historical conflicts transposed on the board of a strategy game. Sultan's adventurous life turns sadly towards a destiny where karma, Hindu myths, and resignation come together in a poetic and reflective way."
BRUNO ELPIS, blogger

## Praise for A Devil Comes to Town

"*A Devil Comes to Town* blew my mind—think Yorgos Lanthimos directing *The Master and Margarita*—it's a bizarre slice of Alpine magic realism that deserves to be everywhere."
*The Observer*

"*A Devil Comes to Town* is a brilliant form of torture—a huge amount of fun."
*The Literary Review*

"This nested narrative is an entertaining exploration of the manifold powers—creative, confessional, corrupting—of fiction."
*Publishers Weekly*

"There's a lot to savor in this bleakly satirical novel, from the description of an isolated town teeming with writers of varying talents to a unique spin on the idea of devils (as opposed to the devil) sowing chaos in the world. The nested structure nods to both nineteenth-century Gothic tales and post-modern lit—which in and of itself suggests the sensibility of this narrative of diabolical interests and literary ambition."
*Words Without Borders*

"*A Devil Comes to Town* is a brilliant form of torture, a perfect nugget of uranium: Maurensig leads us to the question, dangling it like bait, then reels in, packs his belongings, and just goes."
*The Literary Review*

"Maurensig gives us a masterfully constructed gothic horror story designed to keep aspiring writers up at night. A macabre little Alpine horror story elevated by masterful storytelling and language."
*Kirkus Reviews*

"A fabulous take-down of the literati, with a blending of fiction, reported rivalries, and real-world suspicion. *A Devil Comes to Town* is a captivating, clever, and deliciously teasing little tale."
*Never Imitate*

"Maurensig highlights the traps in the desire for literary fame and the resultant money. Only a spoilsport would disclose the ending of this moral fable that makes fun of the scribblers of banalities, but also examines evil that is frightening because it is contagious—like the rabies spread by invading foxes whose cries are heard at crucial moments in the narrative. It wouldn't be a Maurensig if the entertaining fable did not have dark seams."
*Sydney Morning Herald*

"Maurensig has created a gripping short novel that is critical of the realities of publishing, a hybrid of at least two genres, highly imaginative, and involving even beyond the final page."
*Critica Letteraria*

"Biblical, oblique, and lying somewhere between thriller, fantasy, and legend, the new novel by Paolo Maurensig, *A Devil Comes to Town*, is a disturbing reflection in narrative form concerning the darker side of writing."
*Il Giornale*

"Paolo Maurensig gives us a refined and engaging literary fable on narcissism and vainglory, and also on our inextinguishable thirst for stories."
*Q Libri*

"Paolo Maurensig skillfully mixes bizarre narrative with great truths about the human soul."
*GraphoMania*

•

**Praise for The Lüneburg Variation**

"Not since *White Knights of Reykjavik*, George Steiner's riveting account of the 1972 world championship match between Boris Spassky and Bobby Fischer, has a writer demonstrated such stunning insight into the nurturing madness that compels chess play at the master level."
*Publishers Weekly*

"An absorbing story, lushly draped in Middle European tragedy, one blending the themes of obsession, history, and character."
*New York Times*

"A masterpiece—a profound metaphysical thriller about vengeance and justice."
*Los Angeles Times Book Review*

"Not only a riveting read, but a memorable one."
*People*

## Praise for Canone Inverso

"Mesmerizing narrative, a tour de force."
*Publishers Weekly*

"Highly recommended wherever good literature is read."
*Library Journal*

"Maurensig explores the inexplicable variations of human behavior. The man is assuredly a master."
*Los Angeles Times Book Review*

"His second novel, *Canone Inverso*, displays many of the same qualities of *The Lüneburg Variation*: an intricately wrought plot, with stories-within-stories and unexpected inversions and reversals, narrated with a crystalline clarity that makes the novel, for all its complexity, not only easy to follow but hard to put down."
*Wall Street Journal*

"Maurensig has created a masterpiece of mysterious tragedy and lingering shadows, a compelling story with a shocking and enlightening ending. This stunning novel examines relations between father and son, the impact of political chaos on the arts, and the human quest for both literal and metaphorical immortality. Maurensig's brilliant

storytelling, in which the characterizations are compelling and the timing perfect, makes this novel of desperate intrigue and artistic passion one of the best reads of the year."
*Booklist*

•

**Praise for Theory of Shadows**

"*Theory of Shadows* uses the game of chess as a vehicle to meditate on the Holocaust—in the brilliant darkness of his story, Maurensig investigates the cost of complicity with evil."
*World Literature Today*

"In this slim yet complex novel, Maurensig returns to themes familiar from his debut, *The Lüneburg Variation*: fascism and chess. In 1946, world chess champion Alexander Alekhine was found dead in his hotel room in Portugal, the official cause listed as choking on his dinner. The scene screamed cover-up, and Alekhine's life provided a bevy of murder motivations."
*Booklist*

"Furst meets Nabokov: an atmospheric blend of historical fact and detective-tale speculation against the backdrop of international chess."
*Kirkus Reviews*

# Game of the Gods

Paolo Maurensig

# Game of the Gods

Translated from the Italian
by Anne Milano Appel

WORLD EDITIONS
New York, London, Amsterdam

Published in the USA in 2021 by World Editions LLC, New York
Published in the UK in 2021 by World Editions Ltd., London

World Editions
New York / London / Amsterdam

Zwaan Lenoir, Wormerveer, Netherlands

*British Library Cataloguing-in-Publication Data*
A catalogue record for this book is available on request from the
British Library.

ISBN 978-1-912987-14-6

First published as *Il gioco degli dèi* in Italy in 2019 by Giulio
Einaudi Editore S.p.A, Turin

Twitter: @WorldEdBooks
Facebook: @WorldEditionsInternationalPublishing
Instagram: @WorldEdBooks
www.worldeditions.co.uk

Book Club Discussion Guides are available on our website.

This novel makes no claim to being a biography of Sultan Khan. The episodes of the life of the great Indian chess master, and of his brief career, are partly true and partly imagined. They are the inspiration for a narrative schema, consequently any references to people and places—that are not documented—are to be considered purely coincidental.

There is no doubt that modern chess can claim to be directly descended from the ancient war game *chaturanga* that was conceived in India at the dawn of time and later spread from Persia to Europe. There—by then stripped of its sacred character—it took root permanently, thanks in part to the establishment of an international federation that stamped it with precise features and definite rules, without which it would not have been possible to make it the subject of study. Only its codification, in fact, has enabled the infinite possibilities and chess combinations to be thoroughly explored.

As in all manifestations of human thought, the history of this game is studded with bizarre personalities whose brilliance often crossed the line into madness. Many of them contributed to the theory of openings, leaving an indelible mark in the annals, while others staked everything on their innate talent, obtaining extraordinary personal results, only to then disappear from the panorama of chess altogether. Among these was only one Asian player, from India, whose real name was Malik Mir Sultan Khan.

The life of this extraordinary figure seems to be something right out of the pages of Kipling.

But the luminous trail that Sultan Khan left in the chess firmament is that of a shooting star: a dazzling radiance that precedes the most utter darkness.

If it were not for the testimony he himself gave to *Washington Post* correspondent Norman La Motta, on the eve of war between India and Pakistan, we would not know anything about him other than the games documented in various tournament records of the time.

## FROM THE NOTEBOOKS OF NORMAN LA MOTTA

# 1

In 1965 I was in the Punjab, sent by the *Washington Post* to cover the developments of a difficult diplomatic negotiation that was drawing India and Pakistan towards the abyss of a bloody conflict. At the moment, however, the situation seemed to be at a standstill: news was scant and no one could predict how much longer the respite would go on. For some weeks I had been staying in a hotel in Delhi, along with about thirty colleagues from other countries. The air was heavy, electric—monsoon season was coming up—and we reporters spent the day formulating hypotheses, drinking beer, and playing cards.

The waiting became more and more enervating day by day, and by then I had reached the point where I could no longer stand that state of vitiating dejection. Fortunately, I found a way out of it. What drove me into a seemingly fruitless venture was a comment overheard in passing while we were at the table. The speaker was a Belgian journalist, a veteran, known for his many years of experience in "oriental matters."

"The weak point," he said, "the one that will suffer the greatest repercussion from this conflict, will be the border that passes through Mittha Tawana."

And it was the name of that place, about sixty miles from Delhi, that made me decide to go in search of a certain individual who had been the center of a scandal about a decade ago in New York. Finding a man who has been missing for years in a region as vast and populous as India is already a difficult undertaking in itself; it becomes hopeless on the eve of a war. Yet I felt confident.

To get a clear idea of the circumstances, however, it is necessary to go back in time. The man I was looking for was an Indian who in the mid-Fifties had unwillingly been thrust into the bleak limelight of world attention, suspected of having defrauded an elderly American billionairess, a blind woman, moreover, in order to gain possession of her assets. What drew my attention to that grotesque affair at the time was the prestigious name of the accused suspect: Malik Mir Sultan Khan.

"It must be a coincidence," I'd told myself. The name was, in fact, also that of an idol of my youth. As a boy, like so many of my peers, I had been a chess enthusiast, and I had my chosen darlings; among them, Sultan Khan had been my favorite. The fact that he came from mysterious India, traveling under the protection of an authentic maharaja, had only fueled my adolescent fantasy.

Finally, the surprise: it was the very same person! There was no doubt whatsoever. The confirmation had been handed to me by a brief press release: the Sultan Khan who had been pilloried by the scandalmongering press had been a great chess champion in his youth. But for readers eager for risqué details, that fact had gone unnoticed.

At the university and later in the years to come I had tried to reconstruct the life of that individual, with the intent of writing his biography. With that story *in pectore*, I had subsequently even entertained the idea of winning a Pulitzer. But his tracks had been completely covered, and although I'd sent dozens and dozens of letters to the editorial offices of various chess magazines, I got nothing in return. Then, after vanishing from London even before the Second World War, he reappeared again, after ten years, more than three thousand miles away, in the city of New York.

At the time I'd been elated. It didn't seem possible to have found him again after such a long absence. All I had to do was wait for the clamor around his case to quiet down so I could go see him and have him tell me his life story personally, word by word. But things did not turn out the way I had hoped, because, once the curtain had been lowered on the tragicomic episode featuring him as protagonist, Sultan Khan disappeared again.

And now that I was only sixty miles from Mittha Tawana, the village where he'd been born, I thought that I would never again have such an opportunity to contact him in person, or at least find someone who could put me on his trail. I therefore informed my colleagues that I would be gone for several days, asking them to collect any messages left for me. They tried in every way possible to dissuade me from leaving the hotel; it was not at all sensible, in fact, to go wandering around a territory that was literally a powder keg ready to explode. But by then I was prey to the fascination that India holds for Westerners. I felt that everything was possible and that I had nothing to fear. The word *karma*—a term hitherto overlooked—assumed significance in my mind, and I was already convinced that I was there for the sole purpose of tracking down that man. I had never been able to tolerate the fanatics of oriental philosophies; I had always felt slightly irritated hearing anyone talk about chakras, nirvana, karma ... Here, however, I found myself in a different dimension, with precise parameters: the word karma was an excellent substitute for Western terms such as destiny, fate, nemesis, or what have you. It was like the taste of a local wine that is preserved intact only in the place where the vine that produced it grows.

In past years, I had already collected quite a bit of material about Sultan Khan: photos and articles taken from newspapers dating back to the Thirties, when he had arrived in Europe in the service of Maharaja Sir Malik Umar Hayat Khan. After four years of successful matches, however, his career was suddenly interrupted, and once he'd left the circuit of the great international tournaments, he'd been quickly forgotten. No one knew what he might have done in the meantime, and had it not been for the "scandal" related to the legacy of Cecilia Abbott, one of the wealthiest women in America, who died in "mysterious circumstances," nothing more would have been known about him. At the time, in fact, sensational tabloids such as *Confidential*, *Hush-Hush*, and *Whisper* had repeatedly hounded the man, describing him as an impostor, an unscrupulous opportunist who supposedly induced a trusting eighty-year-old widow to marry him so he could get his hands on her considerable fortune. The most outrageous hypotheses had arisen around the case—even one suggesting that he had hastened the elderly woman's departure, replacing the drugs prescribed by her personal physician, and treating her with the laying on of hands, or with who knows what diabolical potion. It must be remembered that at that time the nation was going through an extremely delicate moment: after saving the world from the Nazi boot heel, the Americans seemed prey to schizophrenia, and saw dangers of all kinds lurking everywhere. No sooner had the bogeyman of Communism eased, after spawning the baleful McCarthyist inquisition, than a new and more subtle threat to American respectability began to appear on the horizon. A threat that was as yet nameless, but noticeable in people's conversations: everywhere people gathered the topics turned to free love, yoga, natural cosmetics, and weight-loss diets. Young people belonging to the well-to-do middle classes became fascinated by the very first "flower children." In a short time, scions of billionaires would repudiate their parents and their wealth in order to wear orange robes and go around singing the praises of Krishna. This seemingly innocuous madness soon infected older people as well, who, regardless of their heirs, would contribute generous sums to some sect or other whose ideals were not always exemplary, declaring themselves willing to give up their possessions to follow the guru of the day who would lead them to nirvana. These were still sporadic cases, warning signs, but for conventional types the danger by association was the Indian, the guru capable of duping the masses and making them lose their devotion to the god of money. Thus, the little dark-skinned Indian immediately became the scapegoat of a bigoted, narrow-minded America. And for the tabloid press, the case in which Sultan Khan was involved was too delicious a morsel to let slip away so easily.

I did not have any auspicious clues for finding the man—assuming he was still alive—but I felt I had to put aside any feelings of hesitancy and let myself be guided. But by whom or what? By one of the many deities that India was teeming with? By instinct? Or by the very essence of the person I was looking for? The important thing was to keep an open, receptive mind, assuming a purely Eastern mentality, and groping my way in the hope of finding someone who might set me on the right path. Besides, I didn't even know what he looked like at the moment: I might very well come across him without recognizing him.

I began my search at his place of birth. But if at the start of the century Mittha Tawana was still a rural settlement inhabited by a few thousand souls, now it was part of a district whose population was a hundred times greater. I accomplished little or nothing there, but all in all, karma was not hostile to me. After traveling more than three hundred miles in an old rented jeep, retracing the same routes over and over again, often at the back of endless columns of military transports, and just when I was in fact about to give up, I met a person who put me back on track. She was an elderly Indian doctor who, from the description I had given her, was sure she had met him not long before in Sargodha, in the hospital of a mission of Comboni priests.

My search seemed to be leading me back to a spot not far from where I had started.

I had no trouble finding the mission, which was known to everyone within a few miles' radius. Comprised of a garnet-red building that stood near the road, it had been erected in the lee of a centuries-old banyan, a sacred tree for the Indians, a gigantic specimen that, judging from the circumference of its trunk and the hundreds of grotesquely entangled roots, had to be much older than the mission itself.

I had barely closed the car door before dozens and dozens of monkeys already began warily climbing down from the tree branches. The nun who came to let me in seemed equally wary. When she heard I was looking for Sultan Khan, she gently closed the door in my face without saying a word. I had to wait fifteen minutes before the door opened again. The prior who came to receive me did not seem happy with this unexpected visit, and, at my renewed request to speak with Sultan Khan, demanded to know the reason for my interest. There was the chance that I might be taken for the usual unscrupulous reporter. So I got by with a half-lie: I said that I was writing an article on the situation of those who, born and raised along the Indo-Pakistani border, were in danger of suddenly finding themselves in a territory with a Muslim religion. The addition of a ten-dollar bill convinced the prior to act as intermediary. The fact remained that the final decision was up to Sultan Khan, who at first categorically refused to see me. I had come too far, however, to return empty-handed; so I settled down in the waiting room, determined not to leave before I spoke to him.

Little by little, as time passed, the details of the story that had implicated him came back to me.

It had all started with the reading of the will of Cecilia Abbott, one of the wealthiest women in America, from which it appeared that, before dying, the billionairess had bequeathed a renowned stranger the usufruct, for the duration of his natural life, of her luxurious penthouse with a view of Central Park; besides that, and in addition to a monthly stipend, she'd left him a Rolls-Royce Silver Dawn convertible. The only request in return was that he take care of the two household pets: a Persian cat and an Indian parrot.

From a purely legal standpoint, there had been no grounds of any kind to be able to challenge the will. The judge ruled that the beneficiary could enjoy the use of the penthouse as long as he lived there on a permanent basis and took care of the two pets, or rather, only the parrot, because after a few days the cat had decided to follow her mistress. On the other hand, there were no conditions of any kind on the bequest of the Rolls convertible. This was attested to by a handwritten letter from Mrs. Abbott, attached to which was a document transferring the property, requiring only his signature.

After a few hours, Sultan Khan acceded to my request and agreed to receive me. It was a small victory that I could not afford to waste. I would have to act cautiously, avoiding any missteps; he must certainly not view journalists kindly, and a single wrong question might reopen old wounds. Given these prerequisites, getting him to talk about himself could prove to be a difficult under-taking.

I was taken to the first floor, to the infectious diseases ward. A nauseating smell of slops, mixed with a medicinal odor, permeated the rooms. The nurse pointed to the door and advised me not to tire him too much.

When I entered his room, I found him sitting on the edge of the bed, wearing a pair of striped pajamas. Emaciated, gaunt, with a sunken face marked by an unkempt beard, and long white hair that contrasted his dark complexion, Sultan Khan was a man who appeared to be around seventy. In reality he was ten years younger, but was debilitated by the illness he'd been suffering from for a long time, and which lately had worsened. I was advised, in fact, to keep a handkerchief in front of my mouth if I got too close to him, because tuberculosis in its advanced stage becomes most contagious. He welcomed me cordially, yet avoided shaking my hand when I held it out to him. He seemed apologetic for making me wait so long.

"How did you find me?" he asked with a touch of resignation in his voice. "I thought I had completely covered my tracks."

Unlike what the newspapers had said, he expressed himself in good English, with a pronunciation typical of the Indian middle class.

"It wasn't easy," I said. "I had the good fortune

to meet someone who put me on the right trail."

"Which magazine do you work for?"

"I'm here as a war correspondent. I work for the *Washington Post*. I took advantage of the opportunity to meet you. I also wrote you some letters in the past."

"There are people who hound me because they believe I have paranormal powers. I had to contend with them just after the war and I assure you that they have never stopped looking for me … You must have heard about my health, I suppose."

I said that I had.

"Well, I would like to avoid spending the little time I have left shut up in a cubicle, serving as a guinea pig with electrodes in my brain, and with mountains of questionnaires to fill out."

He immediately made it clear that an interview was out of the question. How could I blame him? I tried to convince him by solemnly promising him that ours would simply be a conversation, and that I would not ask about events he did not want to talk about. Furthermore, none of it would get out without his consent. But despite every attempt, he remained adamant. It was only when I confessed to him that as a young man I had been a great admirer of his that he changed his mind. I also told him that I would like to assemble his memories in a book, contributing the proceeds however he chose.

My proposal seemed to stir a certain interest in him.

"So as a young man, you were a chess fan ..."

"I followed all your matches."

"Really?"

"At that time you were my idol," I confirmed.

He gave me a sidelong glance to make sure I was telling the truth.

"I could agree to speak to you only under several conditions ...," he said uncertainly, as though conflicted.

"Anything you say."

I saw that it was not the prospect of gain that convinced him, but rather the idea that his life might be told in a "book," as if only books could relate the truth.

"By now the newspapers have said everything about me that could be said, except the truth. The first condition that I place on you, therefore, is that you fill this gap. If you promise to be sincere I will tell you every detail of my life, and describe how karma has acted on it since childhood. The second condition is that you not let anyone know where I am, at least not as long as I am alive."

"You have my word."

Sultan Khan rose from the edge of the bed and went to a table that stood beneath the lazy rotating blades of a ceiling fan. With a gesture he invited me to sit down. Between us was the entire length of the table. When, along with my notebook, I also took a tiny tape recorder out of my bag, I noticed his look of surprise. At first I was afraid he wouldn't want to be recorded, but instead he was simply intrigued.

I turned the microphone toward him and had him say a few words. Hearing his own voice played back, his eyes widened and he burst out laughing like a child. I was struck to see such a childlike expression spread over the face of an elderly man. It showed a heart free of duplicity, incapable of lying or of hiding his emotions, to the point of being utterly vulnerable.

"Malik Mir Sultan Khan ... is that your real name?"

He nodded.

"To what do you owe such a magniloquent name?"

An uncertain smile wavered on his lips.

"It was a choice my parents made. Ours was a family of farmers, servants of the land: we mostly cultivated sugarcane, and we all worked for the maharaja, Sir Malik Umar Hayat Khan, who was the wealthiest and most powerful man in Punjab. It is a tradition still widespread today to give a newborn child one of the many names of his owner. It does not claim to be a sign of distinction; rather, it is meant to demonstrate submission: by bearing his master's name, the child belongs to him, like an object engraved with its owner's monogram."

"Although for different reasons, your name experienced two periods of notoriety: the first time in London, at the beginning of the Thirties, when you were in the maharaja's retinue. And later in New York, in the service of Mrs. Abbott."

"You cannot say that I was in Mrs. Abbott's service. I was simply a friend, a companion. I was a guest in her home."

"For how many years were you with her?"

"For seven years, approximately."

"Was it a painful loss?"

"The Master teaches us that life is like a drop of dew poised on a lotus leaf; he teaches us not to fear death, because as long as we are able to think about it we are still alive, and when it over-comes us, we are no longer so. In India there is a much greater fear of birth, because it leads us inevitably towards suffering. Every birth is met with a tear, every death with a touch of joy in the heart. We Indians have a different conception of death; we can allow ourselves to feel sorrow over the premature loss of a child—only because by dying he will miss the chance to redeem himself through the cycle of rebirths—but certainly not for that of an old person who has already com-pleted the entire arc of her existence. And Mrs. Abbott, or rather, Maharani, as I called her, was about to turn eighty-nine at the time of her death."

The fact that Sultan Khan had spontaneously decided to speak about Mrs. Abbott eased my conscience: it meant that there had been no coercion, and that the choice of topic was entirely his.

Sultan Khan continued:

"Certainly, losing her grieved me. For me she had been a special woman. A woman who had been able to free herself from the attraction of Maya, the principal cause of our rebirths."

Perhaps noticing my perplexed expression, he felt obliged to elaborate on the subject.

"All the yoga techniques invented over the course of time, and considered by you Westerners to be mere forms of gymnastics, are nothing but attempts to break the inexorable hold that Maya exerts on man's soul. The allure is irresistible, it keeps us bound to matter, existence after existence, in a chain that is difficult to break. It is said that in order to be able to free ourselves from her, we must first be able to recognize her. I've thought about her from the time I was a child. I imagined a female figure, though without being able to picture her completely."

I had the impression that Sultan Khan was completely estranged from reality. His eyes rolled up as if he were dreaming while half-asleep, and from time to time his voice took on an absent, impersonal tone.

I understood that I would have to let him talk without interrupting him, even if it meant having to listen to every religious or philosophical digression of his down to the very last one.

"If there is something that unites and at the same time divides our two cultures, it is the attitude we assume towards death. The West, when it is not completely skeptical about the soul's survival, affords man one life, however brief it may be, with the expectation of eternal reward or punishment. One of the pillars of our religion is a belief in karma, very often confused with the Western expression "ineluctable destiny." The latter leads to the worst fatalism, by which it would be useless to act, since everything is already written in the stars. Nothing could be more wrong!"

At that point he broke off. He seemed to be wondering if he should continue telling me his story. From the road, meanwhile, came the rumble of dozens and dozens of troop transporters, making the mission's walls tremble. I could have encouraged him with some well-aimed questions—we journalists are experts at this—but instead I chose not to intervene, waiting for him to decide whether to continue. The last thing I wanted to do was tire him out too soon, or irritate him. Then, abruptly, I saw him reemerge from his past with a deep breath, as if after a long apnea.

"But let me tell you everything from the beginning!"

## 2

It is not always easy to understand how karma acts upon our lives. As far as I am concerned, if its last manifestation was the meeting with Maharani, I can say with certainty that it was already written from the time of my childhood, when a killer tiger targeted our village.

In reality it was not a tiger, but the embodiment of the most evil being one can imagine. Since the world has existed, in fact, the relationship between man and tiger has always been one of great respect on both sides. An ancient legend maintains that in the distant past man and the tiger were brothers, each distinguished by his qualities: the tiger by its strength, man by his intellect; and this relationship has never failed. The tiger is considered a sacred animal, and its symbol, if worn hung around the neck or sewn in one's garments, is a powerful talisman that protects against all danger. Moreover, a representation of the tiger carved on the floor at the foot of a bed keeps evil demons away, ensuring peaceful sleep. A tiger that is sighted near a village is therefore welcomed as a visit from the goddess Parvati. Offerings are made to it, prayers are said asking that it spare the village's inhabitants, especially the children, and that it be satisfied with choosing only the domestic animals necessary to appease its hunger, after which it is urged to continue on its way. And the tiger, remembering that ancient bond that bound it to man, usually proves to be benevolent, provided it is not attacked with the intent of capturing, or, worse yet, killing it.

Often, however, in order to approach their victims, evil demons assume the form of protective spirits, so that, trusting their appearance, you fall under the illusion that you are opening the door to a bestower of good, when instead it is actually evil that crosses the threshold at our explicit invitation—without which no demon could enter our home. Even the elders of our village were initially deceived and saw in that creature, who was in truth evil, an emanation of the goddess Parvati, the bride of Shiva, who is often depicted on the back of a tiger. Thinking the tiger to be benevolent, the usual prayers were said and ritual sacrifices offered, but it didn't take long for the animal to transform into Parvati's dark counterpart, into the embodiment of the bloodiest goddess in our entire pantheon: the goddess Kali with the long protruding tongue, the harlot, as black as scorched leather, the lascivious dancer, with six arms like tentacles and hips girded by a loincloth of human tibias and skulls. This was the spirit that animated the murderous tiger who for more than a year ravaged our village.

As a result of old age, illness, or some accident that may have limited the agility necessary to hunt, the tiger can view the human being as a prey to keep itself from starving. Usually, these suffering animals bear the signs of their weakness clearly marked on their bodies: gaunt, mangy, toothless, lame ... They pace around the village waiting for a living creature to come within reach, but are also ready to sprint away like a stray cat when a stone is thrown. They can overwhelm an adult only if they catch him by surprise. But this big cat that suddenly appeared at the edge of our village was much larger than normal and showed no signs of physical decline; on the contrary, it was one of the most robust specimens I'd had occasion to see. In fact, I was the first to spot the animal and to dodge its first attack. The initial sighting took place in a dream.

I was fifteen years old and I was the village *carnac*—the elephant watchman. We had three elephants, all of them docile and intelligent, used for the heaviest jobs. My task, besides having to mount and herd them around, was to tend to them, to feed them, and to keep them clean, freeing them from the annoying parasites that wedged themselves into the folds of their thick skin, which in some places was also extremely vulnerable. Being animals of great sensitivity, to avoid sparking jealousy, I had never openly shown preference for any of them, but in my heart I felt a great affection for Suchita, the oldest elephant, which she reciprocated. The animal's shelter—a straw lean-to—was located at the end of the village, a hundred yards from our house, a distance that I sometimes covered in the middle of the night, running to reach Suchita and fall asleep beside her; only at dawn did I return to slip back into the house on tiptoe, without my parents noticing. One night, when I was asleep beside the elephant, I had a dream so real that many hours after I'd woken up it still kept replaying before my eyes. In the dream I was returning home at the first light of dawn, as I had done hundreds of times, when suddenly a tiger loomed up before me—the most frightening tiger I could ever imagine. I woke up shaking all over; it had only been a nightmare, but the air still rang with a resounding vibration. For the human ear, the tiger's roar is a kind of enigma; it rises in the air as if carried on the sonorous current of its own echo. We think that the tiger is a few steps away from us and instead it is hundreds of yards away; or we hear it as though it were a distance away, still in the dense under-growth, whereas it is already about to pounce. I had heard that menacing sound many, many times; as the village carnac, in spite of my age, I had often acted as path-finder for some big-game hunters, and once I had even come face-to-face with a raging tiger. On the back of an elephant I felt safe, but that day the beast had aimed right at me, and would surely have unseated me had it not been deflected by the clout of a pro-boscis, as precise as the slash of a rapier. The tiger had passed so close that I could smell the reek of its cavernous jaws, yet not even then had I felt as much terror as that experi-enced in the dream.

Already I was starting to expect the worst; already I suspected that an evil spirit had assumed the form of a tiger and that it was roaming among the houses of our village at night. And my suspicion grew a few nights later, when Suchita's alarmed trumpeting rose from the elephants' shed. I interpreted it as a signal, as if she wanted to warn me of an imminent danger. I only knew for certain the following day when I led the elephants to the river. Each time it was a delight to watch them roll around where the bottom was deeper, splashing gallons of water on themselves with the full force of their lungs. Usually I sat on a rock, keeping a safe distance from those rollicking clowns because, if I wasn't careful, I could at any moment find myself covered in mud from head to toe. Well, that day, driven as I was by the call of nature, I went off a little way so that I would be hidden from the eyes of anyone who might be passing by. And I soon had the disagreeable feeling that someone or something was crouching in the grass, following me. Abruptly I felt a shiver run through my whole body. I hurried away, returning to the elephants, and at that instant I distinctly sensed a presence moving behind me in the tall grass. I turned around, trying to resist the temptation to start running; although I had been taught not to run in case of dangerous encounters, it was actually instinctive on my part, since I was literally paralyzed. I thought I was done for: the tiger was no more than ten steps away, taut as a spring and ready to pounce. I prayed to all the gods I could think of to grant me the grace to die instantly and not have to suffer too much. Yet there was something strange about the way the animal was hesitating, standing back as if it smelled a trap, sensing I was too easy a prey not to be concealing some danger. Maybe it was my trembling, or the pounding of my heart, but I had the distinct sensation that the ground was shifting under my feet. Unexpectedly, the tiger backed away, finally turning from me and ambling off, grumbling in a huff. Only then did I notice Suchita behind me: she had come to my aid. She wrapped her trunk around my waist, lifting me off the ground, and set me on her back. Lastly, she sounded a warning to the big feline with a blast as deafening as a thousand trumpets. I rushed back to the village to raise the alarm, but no one wanted to believe me. Although I swore I'd seen the tiger up close, all I got was laughter in return. It was no use insisting that Suchita had saved me, since the protests of my fellow villagers only increased, and already there was some name-calling, because joking about certain things brings bad luck. It was my father who came and brought me home, rescuing me from a group of boys eager to teach me a lesson for having dared try to pull their leg. My father, too, was furious; he didn't believe me either, and that night he gave me a taste of his bamboo scourge, an object that I had never seen him use before.

Events, however, did not take long to prove me right. That same night, the desperate screams of a woman woke the entire village: someone had entered the house through the door, which carelessly had not been bolted. Guided by an infallible instinct, the intruder had headed for the crib where an infant in swaddling clothes was sleeping. Feeling himself being picked up, the baby had awakened and had begun to shriek, alarming the parents who, screaming in turn, had managed to chase away the ill-intentioned stalker, whether man, woman, or demon. Fortunately, the long strip of cotton that swathed the newborn had unrolled, letting him drop, completely unharmed, a few yards from the door of the house. Only the following day, in the light of the risen sun, were the tracks identified as those of a tiger.

After that attack, we could be certain that the tiger would not move off before satisfying its hunger. There was plenty of food, and the region was to its liking. This was only the beginning of a relentless siege by an animal that each day seemed to grow in ferocity and cunning.

The vegetation all around the village was largely made up of cotton fields. For the rest it was scrub wood, reeds, and grass as tall as a man; finally, there were the fields of sugarcane, which represented the ideal hiding place for an animal. And those most vulnerable to the danger of attack were the people who lived on the edge of the village, in houses out in the open countryside, like the one in which I lived with my parents.

Meanwhile, the tiger was becoming more and more daring, and after it attacked a young man, dragging him off to the forest where the remains of his body were later found, the pieces torn limb from limb, the elders of the village gathered and decided that the time had come to take action. There was a shadow of deep concern on their faces. They had seen something that they did not dare reveal in what was left of the boy's mauled body: what disturbed them was not the danger associated with an animal driven to kill by a need to appease its hunger—behavior completely in line with its predatory nature—but rather a sign that it belonged to the demonic world, where beings who enjoyed and fed on the suffering of others thrived. The fact that the tiger could be merciless enough to leave its prey alive while devouring it was a thought that kept me awake at night.

Everyone agreed that it was essential to act before the spirit embodied in that beast assumed limitless powers. The first to show their courage were the young men, who the very next day decided to start a hunt. Armed with machetes and a few old muskets dating back to the time of the first Anglo-Afghan war, they set about tackling a task that was not only dangerous, but also far beyond their strength. There was no way to make them see reason, to convince them to come up with a plan that had even the slightest chance of success. Blinded by rage at having seen their friend killed, they wanted only to avenge him. Any conceivable strategy was forgotten, all caution set aside, and it wound up being a kind of frontal assault, fueled solely by the instinct for revenge. Shouting loudly, they threw themselves into the fray, literally into the jaws of the beast, and the hunt, begun with such fervor, ended with four boys wounded and the tiger unharmed. Of all the rusty old muskets that had been assembled to arm a small army, only one had done its job, firing a shot that had missed its target; another had gone off in the hand of the ersatz hunter, cleanly severing his thumb; some of the remaining ones had jammed, while on a few the firing pin had failed to strike. It is well known that uncontrolled fear is transmitted even to inanimate objects, in this case weapons, which inexplicably do not respond; and for a predator's nose the scent provoked by panic is the most intoxicating there is, after that of blood. The tiger had sprung out of a bed of rushes, bringing down four of the young men, then fled into the dense undergrowth. Its claws left deep traces, especially in their pride. The episode would have been much more serious if the tiger had taken advantage of its momentary superiority. Had that happened, few, perhaps, would have been spared.

Afterwards, attempts were made to capture the tiger in a thousand different ways. Sturdy bamboo traps were constructed that not even a dozen men would have been able to demolish, but which were found completely torn apart. Deep ditches were dug and then covered with dry straw—snares that the animal repeatedly avoided. Kali, the man-eating tiger, seemed to have a whole legion of evil spirits in its retinue. For a year it continued to appear around our village, albeit less frequently. Each time it left behind some victims: just like the goddess Kali, it regularly demanded a human sacrifice. Then, for a long time, it didn't show up again. The last time it was spotted, it was so far away that we were convinced it had moved out of our region, or that it had by then been killed by the hand of some skilled hunter. Gifts of flowers and coins were brought to the goddess Parvati in thanks for having put an end to our nightmare. Whereas, before, people barricaded themselves in their houses and did not go out after dusk, little by little they resumed their routines of the past. In the evening, friends and relations stayed outdoors to enjoy the cool air, sitting in front of their houses. And even children were now allowed to roam freely about the village again, without their parents worrying too much about them.

But then, when we least expected it, the tiger returned to terrorize our village. And this time the tragedy struck me personally. My mother was attacked in broad daylight, in the open countryside, while she was loading sugarcane onto a cart. All they found of her were her clothes, torn and bloodstained. As soon as my father heard about it, he armed himself with a rifle and went into the jungle, from which he never returned. I was the only one left. So I took a sharp machete and I, too, headed into the jungle, determined to get justice by my own hands. But someone in the village had noticed my intentions and managed to stop me before it was too late. Certainly, if he hadn't reached me in time, I wouldn't be here to tell you this story. The searches for my parents' bodies were fruitless. In any case, a funeral ceremony was held in their memory, burning their clothing and some personal objects on a pyre. The fact that we had not found their bodies allowed me the illusion, at least, that they were still alive.

Only at this point did the village elders make the decision, so long deferred, of seeking the help of our master: Maharaja Sir Malik Umar Hayat Khan, also called Colonel Umar Khan, or simply Sir Umar Khan.

# 3

Sir Malik Umar Hayat Khan was the largest landowner in all of Punjab. Trying to figure out what his possessions amounted to was like claiming to know the number of stars in the sky or grains of sand in the Thar desert. Suffice it to say that each year his people paid him a quantity of gold and precious stones equivalent to his weight. And no less weighty were the medals and decorations he had earned during his military career, as lieutenant of the eighteenth cavalry of King George V, having distinguished himself on the battlefield on various occasions. Moreover, there had not been a war in which he had not personally taken part. Everyone kept a framed portrait of Sir Umar Khan in the house, which depicted him in full dress uniform. Despite being one of the wealthiest men, if not perhaps *the* wealthiest, in all of India, he was also a well-liked man, just and generous with his subjects, whom he considered family from first to last. Anyone who was born and died on his lands concerned him closely, and he took the matter of the tiger that was decimating his workforce as a personal affront. First he sent some experienced trackers with their hounds to our village, to trace a map of the tiger's movements. The animal ruled over a very vast territory, and from time to time it was reported in other villages, miles away. Some claimed that it even had the gift of being able to be in two places at once, but the two trackers who had come to reconnoiter knew very well the extent to which superstition can influence the minds of common folk, and did not give too much credit to what they were told. There was no doubt that the stalker was the same bloodthirsty animal. It was easy to identify its route; it was more difficult, however, to discern the frequency of its movements.

Some of the elders of our community had

had the good sense to mark the dates of the tiger's appearances on a calendar. One could not be sure, but perhaps the lunar phases might be a common denominator. You only had to compare the dates to realize that its sightings in our village coincided, nine times out of ten, with an approaching full moon.

To the prince's two emissaries, this detail seemed sufficient, and after completing another thorough inspection of the area to search for the animal's tracks, the various directions from which it came, and the spots where it holed up, they left, assuring us that Sir Umar Khan would not be unresponsive to our requests.

Sir Umar Khan was particularly well versed in the use of weapons and in sports that involved physical contact with an opponent. He was a skilled fencer, and also a boxer and polo champion. He had participated in several battles, even sustaining some wounds; one in particular, to the leg, flared up from time to time causing him to limp. Whereas the memories of war were all contained in the innumerable decorations and honors earned during his career, sport became a substitute for the battlefield, and big-game hunting even more so, where a man could use firearms and expose himself to the risk of dying. This was a feature that ennobled the hunt, which would otherwise be reduced to the ranks of dishonorable butchery. What could be better than a tiger hunt for such an individual? Killing that tiger with its legendary powers would nurture his *own* legend. We were sure that he would accept the challenge, and we began counting the days that remained until the imminent full moon of August. When Sir Umar Khan finally arrived at our village, he was welcomed as a blessing. It was a truly rare event for a prince to stoop to personally solving a problem that concerned the sharecroppers of his lands. I have said that Sir Umar Khan was a generous man. It is true that he could afford to be so; nevertheless, others in his place would not have wasted a minute of their time listening to the woes of an underling and would have let him starve to death rather than give him a single crumb of his own bread.

The whole village was jubilant. Hundreds of people cheered him loudly, and weeping women kissed the ground prostrating themselves as he passed. Only one negligible detail darkened the mood of some of the elders: among the many colorful costumes worn by the trackers, one khaki colonial outfit, worn by a white hunter with a cork helmet on his head and a Browning carbine on his shoulder, stood out in all its lackluster monochrome drabness. The Indian prince had invited his British friend to a tiger hunt, and this matter was criticized by a number of villagers who did not look too kindly on Britain's meddling in our country. But, as I would later discover, the relationship between the prince and the British colonizers was rather complicated, fueled by conflicting feelings.

Just outside the village, in an area where the tall grass had been closely razed, a military-style camp was set up: two twin pavilions in the center, one for Sir Umar Khan, on which the Indian flag flew, and one for the hunter, in the shadow of the Union Jack. All around them were the tents of the trackers, servants, and cooks, and the rest of the entourage.

There was no hope that all these people who had suddenly arrived might scare the tiger. It was unlikely that it could be driven away, even with a deployment of forces worthy of a pitched battle. If it really was possessed by one or more evil spirits, I could hardly believe that it would become an easy quarry. Ten days passed before the tiger showed up, and it happened when we weren't expecting it.

Making the most of the wait, Sir Umar Khan had decided to spend his time for the good of the village inhabitants, allowing a representative of each family to come and express their grievances and requests. Some needed a draft animal, some a wagon, others wanted an extension on paying their tributes, and so on ... A line of men and women of all ages had formed in front of his tent, waiting night and day to be received by the master. I, too, had the privilege of being brought before him. With the loss of my parents, I had suffered the most damage. It was my grandfather who brought me to him, though by then he was ill, and unsteady on legs that had become skinny and stiff like bamboo canes. The prince asked me straightforwardly if I had any particular wish to be granted, and I told him I wanted to see the tiger reduced to a doormat.

"That is everyone's desire," said the prince. "I want to hear a wish that concerns only you, and that you have always kept in your heart."

"I would like to take my grandfather to a hospital where he will be treated," I said.

"That is your wish," the prince replied, "but it does not correspond to the natural laws, which must be respected. His life by now is like a dry leaf. To some extent, your grandfather has already departed; all that is holding him to this world is a drop of lymph left in the leaf stalk; when this dries up it will be enough to cause the leaf to fall from the branch."

Like the genie in the lamp, the prince then asked me to make a third wish. And I had—without a doubt—a wish that was all mine, that I never thought I could have come true.

"I would like to learn chaturanga in depth," I said with a boldness I didn't know I had. And, in fact, becoming a champion of chaturanga was the thing I most desired in the world. From the time I had been initiated into the mysteries of this game, my mind had been unable to find anything so magnificent to apply itself to. It was my father who taught me the first moves, and since he could not afford to buy a game board, he had tried to make one using painted cardboard and sandalwood pieces. My father, however, was far from having the skill of a good craftsman, and his hands were better suited to working the land than to carving wood.

The prince was unfazed, but I knew for certain that I had spoken the magic word. As I have already pointed out, Sir Umar Khan was an enthusiast of any sport that required physical competition with an adversary, but chaturanga, on a mental level, was as close to war as one could imagine. And that he was an enthusiast of this game was known to everyone.

"I will be happy to fulfill your wish, as

long as you prove to me that you can hold your own against me."

And so, while the line of petitioners patiently waited their turn outside the tent, the prince had a precious chessboard brought to him. Before we started playing, we both recited the propitiatory formula: *You who have the advantage, You who play and win without fail, Apsara! You who grant victory, I invoke you, Apsara! You who dance with the dice, and cast the lucky toss, may You win the stakes for us, grant us victory with your magic! You who toy with us in the game causing pain and anger in those who lose, intriguing, enchanting Apsara, I invoke you!*

Few people knew this formula. Usually, before starting the game, they simply kept silent for a minute or two, with heads bowed and hands clasped.

The prince was pleasantly surprised. "Who taught you to recite these words?"

"It was my father who taught me the basics of the game. And also this prayer."

Then we started playing. The throwing of a die—the only concession to chance—was favorable to Sir Umar Khan, indicating that the first move was his. Soon we were both so caught up in the game that we forgot all about the world around us. The sun traveled through its entire celestial arc, night came, the villagers lit fires to warm themselves against the cold and set up improvised shelters as they remained waiting patiently. And while, inside the tent, on the mother-of-pearl chessboard inlaid with gold, the master was increasingly dominated by his servant, the terrifying roar of the tiger was suddenly heard, saving the prince from the embarrassment of having to surrender. Sir Umar Khan, in fact, leaped to his feet and, grabbing his rifle, left the tent to be swept away by people fleeing in terror. Even the white hunter with his Browning looked like a bush rooted on the bank of a flooded stream. In the midst of the confusion that had been created, all he could think to do was fire a few shots in the air. A tiger always fears the sound of firearms, recognizing the danger; as it fled into the brush, however, the animal did not miss the opportunity to mark his passage by gravely wounding one of the sharecroppers.

There was not a minute to lose. By then the tiger was too close to let it get away. It had already entered the dense undergrowth, where it felt safe, but had not yet reached the jungle. For certain it was crouched in the tall grass, watching our movements. In less than an hour the forces were reorganized and the field left in the hands of the expert hunters. Having identified the area in which the tiger was presumably hiding, two columns of trackers set out in that direction just before dawn. They seemed to be moving away but were actually surrounding the animal in a pincer maneuver. The plan was to surround the perimeter, cut off the beast's possibility of retreat, and drive it towards a point some distance away from the forest to preclude any means of escape: forced to head into the open fields, it would be an easy target for the hunters. The reasoning was flawless. Nevertheless, it often happened, in chaturanga as well, that an action performed perfectly in one's mind failed in the face of the unpredictability of the opponent's moves. Meanwhile I had remained near Sir Umar Khan's tent, ready to take refuge and shut myself inside if any danger should arise. For a long time in the dark of night I followed the luminous trails left by the trackers' Bengal lights, and listened to the desperate barking of the hounds as they moved away. A shot was heard, followed closely by another, and finally by the characteristic sound of the Browning rifle ...

Sir Umar Khan and the British hunter returned when the sun was already high. Their disappointment was painted on their faces: our master concealed his frustration behind a stony expression; his British friend, muttering curses under his breath, seemed to have it in for his carbine. By now it was clear that the hunt had turned out to be a failure.

Sir Umar Khan remained for another week, so he could hear the last of his sharecroppers' requests. Every wish was granted, except mine. Perhaps the request I made to him seemed too peculiar, perhaps I had disrespected him by committing the sin of pride ... I came up with a thousand conjectures without reaching any conclusion. The fact is that Sir Umar Khan left without giving me an answer. After his departure the tiger did not show up again. Most of the villagers were convinced that, faced with that deployment of forces, the animal had preferred to choose another hunting ground, one that was less dangerous. Some maintained that it had fled unscathed and that, once the waters quieted down, it would return more savagely than ever. Others instead were sure that it had hidden in the jungle after being wounded, and had died shortly thereafter. Only I kept thinking that the tiger was a pawn of karma, meant to enable me to meet the prince, and that, once its task had been accomplished, it would not return again. While everyone in the village had been granted what they'd asked for from the prince, I could not resign myself to the fact that Sir Umar Khan had gone away leaving our conversation up in the air. Still, I had not yet given up. The flame was little more than a hope that was beginning to falter, but it had not yet been completely extinguished.

I went back to working the land, redoubling my efforts because my grandfather was at the end of his strength; that drop of lymph had by then dried up completely. One morning I found him dead, crouched on a mat in prayer position, with his face already covered by flies. That same day his body was taken to the field where bodies were burned. That doleful place, to which I would never have wanted to go, either by day or by night, was far enough away from the village that the stench of burned flesh would not reach the houses. It was in a cove of the river, which stood ready to receive the charred mortal remains along with unburned body limbs, now food for fish and crocodiles. At night, a strange noise rose from there: the same sound that sugar makes when trampled underfoot, but in this case it was an incessant crunching, caused—one would have said—by the boots of an entire army on the march. It was the chomping of the jaws of thousands of rodents that invaded the area at dusk to feast on what was left of the bones of the dead.

I would have preferred not to attend the ceremony, but I was his only relative. The cadaver was placed on a pile of dry wood that was then set on fire. I was forced to follow the phases of dissolution with my own eyes: the body coming apart, various internal organs bursting one by one, leaving nothing to the imagination. In my heart I thanked the gods for having spared me the pain of seeing the bodies of my parents, or what had remained of them, burn.

Left alone, I would not have been able to carry on what had once been the family business. Fortunately, I had relatives in the village who tried to give me a hand, but it would not last long: even with their help it was difficult to reach the quota assigned to me. After my grandfather's death, I was forced to cede the land to the relatives, and I started working for them. As a result, I found myself in a state not much different from that of a beggar, because while it is true that I had enough to eat and a roof over my head, my condition precluded me from any possible future aspiration. And, in fact, that night in Sir Umar Khan's tent, when I gave him a taste of my skill at chaturanga, the hope had been kindled in me that he might grant the wish that I had expressed at his request. By then I knew the technique, but I lacked the guidance of a master able to refine my sensibility. It was not long, however, before I received a visit from an emissary of the prince, who informed me that I should follow him because Sir Umar Khan wanted me at the palace. And so once again karma caused my life to veer abruptly.

**4**

That was how I came to move to Delhi, to enter the maharaja's court as a servant. Going from the humble clay and bamboo hut, where I had lived until then, to the magnificence of his residence seemed like a dream to me. All my miserable clothes were replaced with silks and fabrics ablaze with bright colors. I no longer moved amid the dust and dung of the poor village in which I was born, but in the midst of unimaginable luxury. Sir Umar Khan's attendants—generally young boys from age fifteen up—did not have specific duties, but had to be able to anticipate his every need or desire: to bring him a thirst-quenching beverage at the right time, arrange a pillow behind his back when he felt uncomfortable, or cool him with a fan when he appeared to be suffering from the heat. They had to be able to shave him safely with a razor without bloodshed, brush his jacket and polish his shoes when he wore European-style clothes, and at other times dress him in Indian garb from head to toe, including a turban that had to be taut, trim, and symmetrical. My tasks, by comparison, were quite insignificant: they consisted of making tea and serving fruit at the table. Only at times when my master was having dinner with his guests, did I have the job of cooling the air with a complicated contraption.

When there were no guests at the palace, Sir Umar Khan read, or collected his thoughts in prayer. Sometimes he climbed on a horse and stayed away for days. More often he withdrew to his rooms. He was a restless spirit, ill-suited to living in peacetime. Two or three times a week a man about his age came to see him, and together they spent long hours playing chaturanga, oblivious to everything around them, in a contest on whose outcome the destruction or salvation of the universe itself seemed to depend.

That man was called Kishanlal Sarda and he had been Punjab's champion several times. Sir Umar Khan possessed dozens and dozens of ancient chessboards. Whereas in modern chess, the shape of the pieces has gradually been stylized according to the inspiration of various artisans, the figures of the ancient chaturanga have remained more or less unchanged in form. They can be made of sandalwood, ebony, or rosewood, and it takes a good artisan to carve them. The most precious are covered with a hundred coats of a particularly brilliant lacquer, which requires months, even years, to fully dry. They may be crafted more or less finely, embellished in various ways, polished, covered with gold leaf, and set with stones, but they must always maintain their original form. That which is sacred, in fact, must be able to perpetuate itself firstly in a form perceivable to the eye, because it is from its form—from its mandala—that the power of thought is born.

The two men always used different chessboards, sometimes in mother-of-pearl and lapis lazuli, sometimes in ebony inlaid with gold and silver. So as not to leave finger-prints on the lacquer of the pieces, which the hands' warmth tended to soften, they wore white cotton gloves, the way those handling meerschaum pipes to prepare them for smoking did.

During the games, I would sit next to them on a stiff cushion. My job consisted of pulling a cord that made a rigid shade oscillate back and forth: a rudimentary apparatus to cool the air and keep the flies away. So I found myself close enough to be able to watch them move the pieces on the lavish board. The conduct of the two contenders wholly expressed the oriental spirit: time no longer existed, and the wait between one move and another was left to each player's courtesy. A player should not take so long that it would make his adversary impatient, but neither was he permitted—or at the least it would show a lack of respect—to respond quickly to the other player's move: he had to be able to appreciate its every nuance before responding. Sir Umar Khan made it possible for me to follow the game from up close. And Kishanlal Sarda gave me a few sidelong glances to see by the expression on my face whether at that moment I approved of their play or not. I cannot say for certain, but at times I felt like I was being tested; that the request I had made that fateful night in the prince's tent had been tacitly accepted, but that, since my wish was a special one, it would take time to be able to grant it. Fulfilling someone's wish for a draft animal or a new wagon was easier, but imparting the secrets of the oldest game in the world meant following a more inaccessible path.

Until one day Kishanlal Sarda spoke to me right in the middle of a game. This surprised me, because you weren't supposed to interrupt a chaturanga game unless it was absolutely necessary; questioning me during the game, therefore, meant that the matter was quite serious. I did not hesitate to answer: at that moment the one whose turn it was to move could only save himself by attacking with his elephant. Kishanlal seemed satisfied with my reply and performed the move I had suggested to him. The game then went on for another hour until Sir Umar

Khan surrendered. Immediately afterwards he left us alone and went to his apartments. Kishanlal called me aside and told me of the prince's intention to have me learn the game in depth, both the Eastern and the Western version.

So I began following his lessons, which very often took place even in the absence of the chessboard, and were sometimes reflections on life and human nature. You could not become a top-level player if chaturanga remained simply a pastime. It was the player who had to change, transform himself through study until he was able to access a different reality from that perceived by the five senses. It was not enough for my master to see me win, or find the best move from time to time. He insisted that I be able to comment on the game as it progressed. "Why did you make that move?" he would ask me. And I didn't know what to answer. Sometimes I said that it was just a waiting move, other times that it was a preventive defense, but in reality I was groping about: what my instinct suggested to me did not find a rational counterpart. It was like asking someone painting a human figure why he placed the eyes at that distance from one another, or why the nose is above the mouth and not vice versa. It is in the game's harmony that the pieces must be combined in that way, I thought of saying—to arrange them differently would mean violating an unseen design, leaving events to chance.

My master also began to explain Western rules to me, comparing them with the traditional ones; at first as a matter of simple curiosity, later insisting that I adopt them definitively. There were some very refined ones, such as castling, which gave the king a further chance to protect itself, or even checkmate, which was a less sanguinary way of winning, capturing the enemy king without committing regicide. I couldn't understand why my master wanted to teach me these new rules. So, one day, I got up the courage to ask him:

"Why is it so important to my master that I know how to play the European way?"

"Sir Umar Khan has big plans for you," the master replied, without saying too much. I knew that Sir Umar Khan had already signed me up for the next championship in Delhi, India's most important national tournament, in which the game was played by the ancient rules, but learning the Western ones at the same time seemed to me to be a wasted effort, since I would never go to Europe. Or at least so I thought.

**5**

To play *chaturaji*, an ancient version of chaturanga, requires four players who compete
with one another in pairs: two against two,
like in bridge. Each one moves eight pieces,
and cannot communicate with his partner.
The colors of the pieces are consequently
four: white and black, and green and red,
colors that symbolize the four elements,
and the four castes. But since it is not always
easy to put together four people who are not
only able to master the game at the same
level, but also willing to commit themselves
for an entire day—a single game actually
lasts that long—over the centuries chaturaji adapted to the need to reduce the number of players to two, changing the name to
chaturanga. And it is here that its kinship

with chess becomes evident: the chessboard remains the same, with sixty-four squares, and the two contenders command an army composed of sixteen pieces, exactly the same as in chess. Although the names of the pieces and their movements are different, the strategy remains the same: to try to surround and capture the enemy king. A curious detail of chaturanga is that, in some variations of the game, the piece assigned to make the first move is decided by throwing a die.

With only two players on the field, the number of armies is also reduced from four to two, which means fewer possible combinations, easier to memorize. Moreover, in the Western version, the pieces' freedom of movement is much more fluid.

In fact, even though the name changes to *shatranj, chatranj, chatrang* ... and the chariots become rooks, and the elephants bishops, chaturanga, in its multiple variants, remains the most ancient game played today. Archaeological finds in India date it back to the fourth or fifth century A.D., but according to some scholars, including my master, chaturanga's roots are sunk in legend. It is mentioned in the *Mahabharata* and was supposedly first conceived by the human mind in 3,138 B.C., during a battle between the Kaurava and the Paurava cousins, which took place on the plain of Kuru that extends between the Ganges and the mouth of its tributary Yamuna. The idea of the game is said to have occurred for the first time to Paurava Arjuna, who with his army, composed of thousands of armigers, carts, elephants, and horses, was preparing to attack the no less powerful army of his cousin. Having dismounted, Arjuna had used the tip of his sword to draw a grid of lines on the sandy soil to configure the battlefield, and placed river pebbles on this improvised chessboard to explain to his generals the tactic he intended to adopt in the battle. As he did so, he felt terribly distraught at the thought of having to kill hundreds of men, including friends and relatives, whom chance had enlisted to serve in the enemy ranks; at that moment the idea flashed through his mind that they might lay down their arms if he invented a game capable of replacing a war of weapons with one that did not involve bloodshed. Thus the archetype of chaturanga was initially conceived; later, over the course of centuries, it took shape and spread throughout the world, from Persia to Arabia, and through Spain to Europe, changing its name from place to place.

At one time, however, chaturanga was much more than just a simple war game, it was also a rule to live by. Once upon a time it was the oracle consulted before every major undertaking. For the wise, it was a book of meditation, for the foolish, a lowly tavern pastime. Practicing it correctly meant being as virtuous and enlightened as the gods. Nothing happens on earth that does not correspond to a divine plan, and the masters of a very distant time had understood that play was an insuppressible need of man. Games were therefore the ideal vehicle with which to associate any form of esoteric thought, to perpetuate it for centuries to come and entrust it to the few initiates capable of deciphering its message. In the West this vehicle was represented by the card game, which had its *summa* in the tarot; in the East by board games such as chaturanga. All this was what my master taught me, in addition to the various strategies to adopt on the board. Without this comprehensive, in-depth tutelage I could have become a good player, like many who through study and memorization of the opening moves are able to reach satisfactory levels, but I would never have achieved command of the subject to the point of considering myself a master in turn.

Chaturanga, then, was a game, of course, but also a philosophical text. It embraced the arts, the trades, the religious hierarchy, the social order, and the division into castes. It developed young people's character, whether they were peasants or warriors, it taught them to be patient, to allocate their time among sowing, waiting, and harvesting. It taught the warrior and the commander when it was time to attack and when to retreat. My master would say to me: "When you get to know chaturanga in depth and understand the associations that connect the terrestrial chessboard to the celestial one, you will know yourself and shall then be able to predict the fate of any battle."

At that point, Sultan Khan stopped. He seemed to be about to tell me something extremely important. Then he resumed:

"So then, I would like you to pay close attention to those last words—'You will be able to predict the fate of any battle'—since they mark an important turning point in my life. After a year I had reached the highest levels. I participated in the supreme tournament in Delhi, for which Sir Umar Khan had signed me up; a competition that I won with stunning ease. Despite getting confused at times between the old and new rules, I finished without so much as one defeat. It was then that Sir Umar Khan revealed his intentions to me: he would take me to England to enter me in the national competition, the British Chess Championship. As a subject of the Crown I was fully eligible. From that day on, many things changed: I was relieved of certain domestic duties in order to devote all my time to practicing under the guidance of Kishanlal

Sarda. In addition, European-style clothes were made for me, with knee-hugging trousers, coarse woolen jackets, and even a coat that weighed more than I did. "It's cold in Europe," my master said, "and I don't want to risk having you get sick." I tried them on in front of a mirror. Dressed like that, moreover with a turban on my head, I thought I looked ridiculous. Above all, I thought I would never get used to wearing stiff leather shoes.

# 6

To enable me to familiarize myself with the new rules, Sir Umar Khan had devised a very strange parlor game. As the splendid, generous host that he was, he had guests for lunch almost every week: high-ranking British officers, diplomats, consuls, ambassadors with their spouses ... Pork and wine were abundantly served at the table, and at the end of the meal he did not fail to offer his invited guests a selection of those intoxicating alcoholic beverages so esteemed in the West: cognac and whiskey, such precious distillates that none of them would be able to afford to drink even a drop back in their home countries. Although his religion forbade them to him, on special occasions—that is, when he had guests who belonged to more permissive faiths—he was permitted, by virtue of a rare dispensation, to drink alcohol and smoke all he wanted, provided that the expression on his face did not convey pleasure, but rather a slight hint of disgust. Every transgression had to be later atoned for with an adequate period of prayer and fasting.

Wealth would be a very paltry thing if there were no way to flaunt it. And Sir Umar Khan did not stint on that score: at the end of the meal he gave each lady a pearl or precious stone as a souvenir of the evening, while the men, besides the highly prized liqueurs, were offered cigars specially made with the rarest, most superior tobaccos of the East. Motivating this display was a strong desire to get back at a people that had invaded the land of his forefathers. Although Sir Umar Khan possessed vast, incalculable riches, although he had been decorated with the most sought-after honors, he remained an Indian still, judged by the color of his skin, that is, with a trace of contempt, even by those who professed to be his friends. He was, yes, an ally, yet still in an inferior category. Put into words, Sir Umar Khan's reaction was this: "If you do not accept me as your equal, I will do everything to prove myself superior to you."

In our religion there is a division into castes which is an insurmountable wall, and for those who, like my master, belonged to the noblest caste, it was inconceivable that anyone would presume the right to look down on him. And so Colonel Sir Umar Khan took his revenge, sometimes mocking his own guests. At the end of the lunch, while the ladies visited the gardens with their sparkling fountains and the men, sated, sat there conversing, Sir Umar Khan set the trap for those flaccid, arrogant individuals whom he despised from the very bottom of his heart. With his undeniable oratory skills, he was able to change the subject at will, and when they were all gathered in the *fumoir* he proposed a great challenge. Before getting to the point, he started off by circling around it, with the intention of ruffling his staid British comrades-in-arms by comparing the two cultures. He had no qualms about claiming that Eastern culture was immeasurably older than that of the West.

"Just as India is the mother of all European languages, so it is also the mother of all Western cultures, religions, and philosophies. Even parlor games have their origins in India ..."

At that point many wondered where he was heading with this, but since it was not polite to interrupt the host, they found themselves obliged to put up with the sermon until the end. With the same nonchalance he would have shown if commenting on the weather, Sir Umar Khan sank the red-hot iron into the *amor patriae* of his British guests, going so far as to maintain that Eastern culture was far superior to that of the West, and that this could be deduced from the nature of their popular pastimes, which were, among other things, card games in the West and board games in the East. Some were tempted to argue, but given the host's innumerable citations and honors— conferred by His Majesty King George v for his distinguished service in the British Army, where he had served for over twenty years—the bystanders were forced to swallow the bitter pill with a smile on their lips. My master had a natural penchant for provoking others, but he did so with such civility as to make the other party doubt whether he had understood correctly. To give an example, when a delegation of the British Falconers' Club came to announce that he had been unanimously named honorary president of the most exclusive club in London, the prince received the group of delegates with this singular greeting: "You should feel honored to have been welcomed into my home, because this is usually the hour I set aside to talk to my dogs."

Those words uttered by an Indian, in a territory ruled by the British Empire, was for an Englishman an offense that deserved to be cleansed with blood. Paradoxically, it was too offensive to be understood; a few laughed, some were puzzled: most likely they all thought it was an Indian expression of welcome, impossible to translate.

At times like those, I could understand Sir Umar Khan's state of mind: everything was granted to him, except for one thing, which all his wealth would not have been enough to buy. He had lived in England for a long time, he had studied at Aitchison College and graduated from Cambridge, but he remained an Indian nonetheless, and would never ever be able to pass for an Englishman. And so, due to the well-known compensation mechanisms of the human heart, he ended up scorning that which he had failed to achieve. All his citations and decorations, ostensibly owed to a shameless devotion to the oppressor of his homeland—an affection so excessive as to make him transform the first floor of his palace into an indoor cricket court *for his British friends*—attested instead to a desire to prove himself superior to every son of Albion. And now it was time to counter their arrogance and their brazen sense of supremacy. After offering his guests the choicest delicacies, he enjoyed giving them indigestion. That India was the cradle of every culture was demonstrated not only by its being the locus of the proto-root of all European languages—he claimed—but appeared all the more evident in parlor games in particular, which in the West are frivolous and shallow, very often based on the random toss of dice or the chance dealing of cards. In India, on the other hand, games have far more noble origins, and even more noble aspirations ... And as his guests listened, intrigued, to such pomposity, Sir Umar Khan continued his demolition effort, as if nothing were happening. Nothing showed on his face, but I was sure that for him those were the moments of greatest satisfaction.

"Take chess, for example, which is played by both our peoples: it derives from India's chaturanga, which is at the origin of all board games."

Talking about chess for the English was like touching a raw nerve. In fact, aside from a couple of names, such as Sir George Thomas and Frederick Yates, there weren't many players worthy of note in Britain. As Sigmund Tarrasch, the so-called "father of German chess," maintained, there were no chess masters in Great Britain. It is true that Howard Staunton, who had lived the century before, remained a cornerstone of British chess history, but, more so than to any innovation in the game, his name was linked to the "Staunton pieces," officially approved by him at the time, which were now considered regulation shape and size in all countries. On the ascent to the world championship there were Germans, Russians, even a Dutchman and a Cuban, but to date no Englishman had shown that he was capable of competing. Although there were no cutting-edge diamonds in Great Britain, the game was quite popular even among the lower classes, and on average the level was good, among women as well. Almost all high-ranking British officers had studied at Oxford or Cambridge, the two universities which, since the last century, were considered the most authoritative institutions on matters regarding chess. These true bastions of the game were therefore in constant contention for anything that concerned the theory of openings. It was impossible to have studied at those universities, or attended any military academy, without being at least a mid-level player. Consequently Sir Umar Khan knew that his words would strike someone among his guests, the way a few pellets from a gun, fired haphazardly, accidentally hit the target.

And so, the critical point of his lecture:

"Well then, I can tell you with certainty that the lowliest servant of this palace, a young man who can neither read nor write, would trounce all your so-called champions."

Then, clapping his hands, he invited me to approach. At that I left my contraption for cooling the air and went over with my hands joined and my torso bowed, as befits the humblest of servants. Seeing before them a gangly youth with a somewhat dumb look, who didn't utter a word, many were tempted to put me to the test.

For my part, I knew nothing about chess theory, or at any rate I had no idea of the names of the openings. The ones that for obvious reasons remained in my head were the "Indian defenses," which I tried to adopt whenever possible, in honor of tradition. I had already assimilated the Western rules, which, compared to the Eastern ones, allowed a greater margin for maneuver. And that was enough for me. I regarded with some suspicion the thousands of pages needed to only partially dissect a certain opening, pages that to me seemed intended only to confuse. I thought that if I had to learn chess by going through all that printed paper, I would take up something else. In my mind the moves to be made lit up like lamps along the edge of a shadowy path, along which I walked with ease while others stumbled in the dark. That's all.

My master, however, had cautioned me not to overdo it, not to reveal the slightest satisfaction to my opponent, and, when the game was over, not to try to teach him how he should have played the game—for heaven's sake!—or point out where he had gone wrong. I was simply to say the fateful word "checkmate" and then decorously withdraw. Any analyses and comments were best left to those who had witnessed the game. And so, from time to time, the servant continued to beat the most illustrious of the guests, stringing one victory after the other like pearls on a thread. As careful as I was, I sometimes happened to win too easily, unintentionally wounding my opponent's pride. Many of them, when they realized they had lost, would have gladly shot me point-blank. I think that there is no other game in which defeat proves to be so painful. This is because chess is associated with intelligence, whereas to make a good player, other qualities are required: sangfroid, prudence, focus, tenacity, courage ... without which intelligence counts for very little.

I continued to mow down my victims, undaunted; there was, however, an agreement with my master, who on some rare occasion, with a prearranged signal, would indicate to whom I should concede a draw. It was some influential person whom it was not advisable to publicly humiliate. For those individuals I reserved the "gentleman's draw," a tie between gentlemen. Those who instead challenged me without thinking twice were buffoons who didn't take anything seriously and turned everything into a personal spectacle, just to get a laugh from their buddies. They were people who couldn't care less about the skills and talents of others. In the end, their excuse was always ready, and its tip was dipped in poison: "I will never manage to understand this stupid game."

# 7

In different circumstances Sir Umar Khan's provocations would have called for immediate satisfaction, but it was better not to try anything, given that he was a skilled swordsman and a champion at target shooting. There was no choice but to resort to humor to salvage the situation. Occasionally no one felt like challenging me. To make the confrontation less direct and the defeat less stinging, Sir Umar Khan proposed that his guests form small groups of three or four and play in consultation. That would make the contest more enjoyable, he said. By playing that way, no one would be solely responsible for a defeat, and would be able to attribute the blame to this or that teammate who had earlier suggested the weak move. That way each of them got the feeling that he would have played the game better on his own. And some of them, in fact, asked for a rematch to be played individually. The fact is that many of them, after being defeated, felt so affronted that they no longer wanted to set foot in the prince's house. One of them, I remember, took it so badly that he walked out on the game muttering that he didn't feel like continuing to play against an *idiot savant*. Those words struck me with unprecedented viciousness; never before had I felt so humiliated. I remember that I made an enormous effort to hold back tears. So that was how they saw me: some kind of idiot ... I took that description as an insult—as in fact it was meant to be—and on the day before the usual social gathering I went to bed with the excuse of not feeling too well. I told my master everything, and he tried to comfort me.

"You see, Sultan, that is a typically Western expression meant to disparage a person of genius. For them it is inconceivable to be beaten by you, and this is their natural reaction. Prepare yourself to endure the worst the human heart can express in the future, but do not let your talent weigh on you; you must console yourself with the thought that perhaps in your previous lives you worked hard to reach the level of the game that you now possess. Our talents are revealed from life to life, until even something extremely difficult for others seems as easy as breathing to us."

In front of the chessboard, of course, things are seen in perspective: no one so far had proved difficult for me, there was nothing but a succession of victories on my part. So I returned to my role of "poor little timid soul who plays chess well" with a different spirit: this time enjoying their defeats.

An incident occurred, however, that was neither gratifying nor amusing: an episode that made me seriously doubt the much-vaunted British self-control, and that perhaps hastened my being brought to Europe. One evening, after a lavish dinner accompanied by the finest wines, four skillful chess players gathered, intending to get back at me. The time was right, the wine's effects had stirred their patriotism. Two of these were masters, or at least they said they were. They gave it their all, without success. Having no excuse for their defeat, the most infuriated of the four knocked all of his pawns onto the floor. He was about to smash his fist on the precious chessboard, not thinking of the incalculable damage that he would have caused, except that at that point a certain Major Buchanan, who had witnessed the game, stepped in. After calming everyone down, the officer turned to the prince with these words:

"Your Excellency, I do not know how to play chess. I know the rules, but I cannot say that I am able to play. However, I can confidently say that I would hardly waste my time on a game that frankly seems to me appropriate for idle good-for-nothings. Nevertheless, what you assert, namely that this faint-hearted stripling is capable not only of standing up to, but actually thrashing our greatest British champions, leaves me stunned. Can it be that the confidence flaunted by your excellency derives from the fact that what you claim can be neither disproved nor demonstrated?"

"Are you saying that there is no way to disprove my assertion?" Sir Umar Khan asked in a honeyed tone.

"Precisely, since what you assert cannot be demonstrated."

"Anything can be demonstrated."

"But what you are affirming, namely that this simpleton is capable of winning the British Chess Championship, sounds like an affront to Sir George Thomas and to Frederick Yates, our two titleholders, and I would be ready to wager any amount that if your pupil were to participate in a tournament of that caliber, assuming they were to accept him, he would only come out with his tail between his legs, and go running back to work that is more congenial to him."

This arrogant man, with his toothbrush mustache, his riding crop tucked under his armpit, did not immediately realize that his words were reawakening in my master's soul his devouring secret passion: gambling. Just on hearing the word "bet," Sir Umar Khan's backbone straightened up like a cobra from its basket at the first notes of a flute.

"Wager ... you say: so why don't we make this wager? I'll wager that for my servant to win the British Chess Championship would be child's play."

"I spoke of a wager," the major said with an apologetic smile, "but in reality I realize that a wager between us two is impossible, since there could be no adequate stake. If only there were, believe me, I would not hesitate ..."

Major Buchanan was tightening the noose around his neck all on his own. Sir Umar Khan appeared to be reflecting. Finally he asked:

"How much do you weigh, major?"

"Come again?"

"What do you weigh?"

"About two hundred pounds," the major replied, still not understanding that odd question.

"I'll bet two hundred pounds of gold on my servant's victory," said Sir Umar Khan.

Major Buchanan visibly blanched. "If only I had two hundred pounds of gold, have no doubt that I would stand ready to accept your wager. But I do not possess your riches."

"Certainly not," replied my master, "but to me a penny from you is enough, against a value in gold equal to your weight."

Faced with this proposal, Major Buchanan began stammering in disbelief. A few drops of sweat beaded his temples and ran down his cheeks into the collar of his shirt.

It was a tempting offer, all too tempting.

"In that case," Buchanan said, "I could well accept the wager. Nonetheless, it does not seem like a good deal for you. I would not lose anything, whereas you would be divested of a large amount of precious metal, since I would have no intention of reducing my current weight to please you." So saying, he burst into brash, hysterical laughter meant to cover, at all costs, the lack of confidence he was beginning to feel as a result of the nabob's offer.

"There are things far more precious than gold," the prince countered, "and one of them is honor. The penny that I ask of you as a stake must be a unique, personal, and unmistakable object ..."

"And what would make it unmistakable?"

"I would be satisfied if you were to have an

inscription engraved on it."

"What sort of inscription?"

"*Next time, before opening my mouth to judge an Indian, I will bite my tongue. Signed: Major Frank Buchanan.*"

And so at the end of the meal the major had to swallow a dose of gall served up in a gold goblet. Unwittingly, he had accepted the wager, and since at least ten onlookers had witnessed the scene, there was no possibility of backing out. Suddenly he felt absurd; everyone who had followed the negotiation looked at him as if he were a rare specimen. They didn't know whether to admire him for his courage or pity him for his gullibility. He realized at once that he had made a fool of himself, and after draining his glass of whiskey, he took his leave. I would never see him again, like so many of the others, for that matter, who had felt affronted or humiliated in some way. Sir Umar Khan seemed to really enjoy creating a void around himself.

**8**

On March 15, 1929, we set off for England following the ancient spice route. Also with us was Kishanlal Sarda, who would act as my second, my trainer, and my interpreter as well.

Sir Umar Khan loved to be surrounded by luxury. Wherever he went, he demanded the best hotel, the best suite, the best cuisine, and the best service. He was always protected by two bodyguards who were able to blend in so masterfully that even I could not spot them among the people who surrounded him. In addition, he was always accompanied by some of his personal servants, I being among them. Although I was his jewel in the crown, on which he would wholly stake his prestige, I was still a servant and treated as such. It is true that I sometimes sat at the table with him, but only when we were alone.

Sir Umar Khan had selected the most spacious cabin, a suite reserved for princes and sovereigns. He could afford it in part because he was the proprietor of that steamer, which belonged to a large fleet that plied the seas all over the world. I, on the other hand, had been relegated to a third-class cabin, which was located in the deepest belly of the ship, right in the midst of the infernal engine noise. Moreover, I had to share the cramped space with Akhik and Avarsh, two brothers more or less my age, who were also in Sir Umar Khan's service. My two traveling companions detested me. They couldn't stand the fact that I enjoyed privileges denied to them just because I could play chess well, and one morning, a couple of days after our departure, I went on deck with a swollen eye and a wobbly incisor. During the night, catching me by surprise as I slept, they had given vent to all their hatred. Ratting is a reprehensible act under any circumstances, so I told my master that I had stumbled and fallen down the iron ladder that led to the lower decks. But Sir Umar Khan was a man of great experience, and since he did not like having one of his goods damaged, he secured a cabin for me on a higher floor, all to myself, leaving my attackers in the hold.

I was not used to traveling. The longest trip I had taken was to Delhi on a cart drawn by oxen. At most, travel for me was represented by the train that passed by our village, whose prolonged whistle could be heard from miles away. It was brought back to me by the ship's siren, which sounded when the vessel approached a port. For us kids, the train was not only the preeminent means of transportation, but a real source of fun. We would wait for it at a spot where we knew that, due to an incline, the old locomotive would slow down before proceeding at a crawl. And that's when the assault began: from the thick underbrush that grew on the sides of the track we rushed out by the dozens, climbing on the footboards, clinging to the handles, clambering up to the top of the carriages, and at each succeeding slowdown other kids joined us, until every last rusty inch of the train was littered with our bodies, transforming it into a very long, colorful dragon. Not tolerating these raids, the railway company had hired vigilantes. But to no avail: even before the train picked up speed, we had all jumped off and disappeared into the thorny vegetation. Many times as a child I had dreamed of continuing on that train and traveling around the world. But now, the mere thought of being so far from terra firma affected my heart and my stomach. A good fifteen days adrift between sea and sky, with a few quick stops that wouldn't even give us time to go ashore—that was what awaited me.

The staff went out of their way to make the journey less tedious, but besides some music and a few performances, there wasn't much to do during the day. There were times when I prayed in my heart that a good, healthy storm might rouse us from that torpor. So when the master Sarda, in accordance with Sir Umar Khan, proposed that the ship's management liven up a day with a simultaneous chess event, the idea was greeted with enthusiasm. Twenty or so tables with chessboards were arranged in a circle in the grand ballroom. It was a seemingly short circuit, but when repeated dozens and dozens of times it amounted to a notable course. I would pause in front of my opponent just long enough to respond to his move, then go on to the next chessboard. The exhibition had its appeal, especially for those who were taking their first steps in the chess world. Sir Umar Khan took advantage of the fifteen-day crossing to make a public showing of my skill. For a final touch, he devised a sitar player to accompany every exhibition with oriental music. Naturally it only took a few laps around for my opponents' ranks to be decimated, until there were only a handful of diehards left, the most difficult to unseat. To them I usually proposed a "gentleman's draw," in this case not to let the game drag on too long and bore the spectators. At the end of the performance, it was not so much my head that hurt me as my feet, squeezed tight in the leather shoes that I still could not get used to.

Among the travelers were some journalists who, intrigued by my ability, wanted to know something more about me and the reason for my trip to Europe. Sir Umar Khan was able to handle the situation, however, and for the time being he did not allow any interviews. Only a few days before my arrival in England did he hold a press conference in which I answered all their questions, satisfying every curiosity and letting the photographers shoot me dressed in traditional garments. Of course, it was Kishanlal Sarda who spoke on my behalf, acting as simultaneous interpreter. He was quite good at maneuvering and avoiding their traps, often inventing his own replies and, in the most extreme cases, resorting to the disclaimer "no comment." After the press conference, several of the reporters present telegraphed their respective editorial offices, and by the following day the news had already spread that a little Indian determined to defeat the best players in the United Kingdom would soon disembark in Europe. Sir Umar Khan knew how to move his pawns in a masterful way: by so doing he created an expectation not only in England, but also in the rest of Europe. He was counting on the fact that after trouncing the British I would be invited to tournaments of a higher caliber and that in a short time I would be able to contend with the great European champions, until finally competing in the world championship. Many wondered—I most of all—what drove him to abandon the comforts he was accustomed to in order to travel far and wide in a cold and hostile Europe. The only answer that came to mind was that Sir Umar Khan, besides being a great enthusiast and patron of the game, wanted to demonstrate the superiority of our people at all costs. Therefore it was extremely important to keep the flame of expectation alive, to create a legend that would encircle my head like a halo. And he succeeded very well in that intent.

# 9

Upon our arrival, there was a crowd waiting for us; the British newspapers had anticipated our coming, some with fanciful headlines, such as "The Turk Brought to Life" or "The Indian Genius." Everyone was intrigued by my great talent that allowed me to compete with experienced masters. They found it hard to believe that I had never opened a chess book in my life. But some hostility could already be read between the lines. I have not forgotten what journalists began fabricating about me from the first moment I set foot on British soil. Was I or was I not a British subject? And if I was, how come I didn't speak their language? All the newspapers, starting with the *London Gazette*, emphasized the fact that although I had a natural gift for playing chess, I was actually an illiterate. And this hurt me deeply. I wasn't really an illiterate, but, according to my agreement with Sir Umar Khan, I had to seem as much like one as possible. My master was convinced that brilliance stood out better against a background of sound ignorance, and to please him I agreed to play the part of a completely ignorant boy. I did not have a solid education, of course— my readings were represented by the *Mahabharata*, my language was Hindi, and I found English rather difficult and chess notation pointlessly complicated—but that did not mean I was stupid. What saved me was shrewdness, wariness, as well as the common sense of a simple man. And that simplicity left me defenseless against the applause of dozens and dozens of people who on other occasions would not have deigned to glance at me. Still, I felt bewildered; I yearned for the tranquility of my village and the life that resembled the placid gait of oxen attached to the plow. All that seemed so far away. It had only been a few years since I had lost my parents, yet I had the impression that a whole lifetime had passed since that time.

Although I had looked forward to my European adventure, now that I was on the battlefield I realized that I had overestimated my physical strength. Maybe because I had never imagined that a world such as that of the great European cities existed, starting with London and its climate, which was especially lethal for those like me who were sensitive to chills. As soon as I set foot in the "land of angels" they had to take me to the hospital to be treated for a malaria attack—a chronic illness that recurred in those times when I was weakest. It was cured just in time with massive doses of quinine. The fever's spasms had been so violent and uncontrollable that I came out of it with broken bones, as if I had tumbled down a stone staircase. Added to the hostility of the climate was that of the city's inhabitants. In the places I came from (I didn't even dare think of being so far away from my beloved India), the worst enemies still exchanged due courtesies, whereas here rudeness and incivility were the norm, even in a place of care and recovery like a hospital. And although Sir Umar Khan lavished princely tips on the nurses so that they would give me special treatment, there was no way to provoke a smile on those perpetually sullen faces. It was immediately clear that a mechanism was triggered in them in which greed and pride came into conflict. The thought that shadowed their faces, even those whose task it was to empty the chamber pots, was: "How dare he, this savage ...?" Sometimes even the most humble of the attendants refused the bill folded in four, held between the index and middle finger in such a way that the offer would seem less offensive.

Another obstacle was the cuisine. People had already warned me, describing English dishes as "cadavers coated with dew." Fortunately, there was no lack of Indian-run restaurants in London, and kosher food was also popular. I found out that Frederick Yates himself, though he was a pureblooded Englishman, suffered from the same ailments as I did: he had a weak stomach and was constantly chilled. Later on, united by these same failings, we ended up becoming friends.

If Sir Umar Khan had not taken me in, I would have been a farmer; instead, everything converged to trace a different destiny for me, consisting of successes but also of inevitable failures. Despite having great prospects for my future, the prince always maintained that distance with me which distinguishes the master from his servant. Except for the rare occasions when he invited me to sit before him for a game, the rest of the time I was his humble servant through and through, just like the other two boys in his service: always ready to fulfill, or better yet, to anticipate his every desire, to scratch his cheek—so to speak—even before the mosquito landed on it. There were times when the player—his secret weapon, who, at least symbolically, would undermine the foundations of the British Empire—prevailed over the servant. But otherwise I was kept at a distance, subject to corporal punishment, obliged to observe silence and reply only when spoken to.

Sir Umar Khan's character was bizarre and unpredictable, not just towards his subordinates. He wanted to show everyone that he was above it all and that he could afford any transgression of societal rules. He liked to make those around him feel uncomfortable, he loved to shock them, to amuse himself at their expense. The following example should suffice. As I've already mentioned, besides the name of my master, my parents had also added that of "Sultan," which often created some misunderstanding. For many of the Englishmen who met me for the first time, *I* was the maharaja, whereas the real sultan, Sir Umar Khan, who generally wore European-style dress, was considered to be an official in my service. This reversal of roles sometimes amused my master, as long as the misunderstanding was quickly cleared up, otherwise it irritated him, especially if it was a journalist who made the mistake. Once, in fact, having invited a dozen eminent figures of the chess world to dinner at his apartment in central London, he had a booklet distributed to the guests, which was printed on parchment paper and portrayed him in full dress uniform on the cover. Inside was his biography along with the very long list of his decorations, medals of valor, and other military and civilian honors. He had never done that before, but that evening he had me serve at the table in a waiter's uniform, which provoked the guests' surprise and disbelief, followed by a general embarrassment that ended up casting a chill over the festive atmosphere. Did he do it just for fun, or did he want to make it clear once and for all that, although I played chess well, I was still his servant? I would never know.

For my part, pride was a feeling that I could not allow myself; my religious upbringing forbade it. I belonged to the Shudra caste, that of servants, after which came the worst of all: the untouchables. It was assigned to me by karma, and I had to accept it as a reward or atonement for how I had acted in previous lives. The more serious the sins that are committed, the more lives are needed to expiate their consequences: to rebel against one's karma is therefore equivalent to prolonging its negative effects. This must be accepted because everything in the universe tends to balance out: the greatest suffering is prelude to the greatest happiness. Moreover, even sultans, princes, and sovereigns are aware of this; they, too, chained to the wheel of existence, know that they can lose their riches and be reborn in a life where they will be servants of their own servants, who have in turn replaced them as masters. So I did not complain. On the contrary, I considered myself fortunate because, if not wealth, I had inherited a talent from my father. I was the true promise of my breeder, like a thoroughbred who seemingly is satisfied with a warm stable and good fodder, but who in reality can't wait to have his competitors taste the red sand of the track.

## 10

We had landed in England in late spring and
the championship was to take place in
August. The maharaja felt it was necessary
for me to become acclimatized before being
able to seriously play in a qualified tournament. It was one thing to play with ama-
teurs, another to compete with champions.
But Sir Umar Khan and the master Kishanlal Sarda had not wanted to rush things and
had made me play in various London clubs
first. It was my master who arranged the
matches for me; he wanted me to become
familiar with the Western rules well before
signing me up for an important tournament, in order to eventually tackle the British Chess Championship. To this end, Sir
Umar Khan, with an attractive pool of prize

money provided out of his own pocket, organized an invitational tournament in London to put me to the test. The result was disastrous: I had to fight with everything I had just to share *ex aequo* last place in the standing. I have only very confused memories of that tournament. That was my European debut. Disappointing? Of course, but I could justify my failure by the fact that I had still not fully recovered from the violent attack of malaria. And in fact, a few weeks later, at the Liège tournament, I redeemed myself by achieving an honorable second place, ahead of champions such as Nimzowitsch, Marshall, Rubinstein ... With a great deal of patience and a true spirit of sportsmanship, Frederick Yates took the trouble to teach me to correctly record the moves on the scorecard, using the British notation. This procedure, essential lest the game be invalidated, remained for me a persistent obstacle to concentration. In addition to the torture of sitting for hours on those three-legged stools called "chairs," not being able to fold my legs, the need to set my opponent's clock in motion each time I made a move also distracted me from the game. Often I forgot to press the button, giving my rival generous portions of time that, added together, forced me to move quickly toward the end of the game during the most critical phases, increasing the chances of making mistakes. Many of my losses, in fact, were due to exceeding the time limits allowed me. Then there were some rules concerning the movement of the pieces that I was still not able to fully assimilate. Castling, for example, a move as bizarre as it was useful to defend one's king, was completely foreign to Indian rules, and as a result it was difficult for me to apply it in the thick of the game. So, very often, following the chaturanga's strategy, which did not include the use of castling, I would leave my king in the center and strengthen both flanks; this gave my opponents the impression that they could easily penetrate my defense, thereby forcing them to expose themselves in turn. Often the commentators were flabbergasted by my unorthodox choices and, considering them weak, noted them with a big question mark, not realizing that they were actually the fruit of another vision of the game, with rules that were different from the presiding ones. Often the players in front of me wasted their time trying to figure out why I had chosen a "weak" move when another one was visibly better. *British Chess Magazine* led into its review of my game this way: *Is it possible that the sum of a series of weak moves can produce a winning position?*

But I would not wish to bore you with these technical details when I don't even know how familiar you may be with the game. So many years have passed since then that the layers of my memory are superimposed on one another. Things that have been forgotten for some time return forcefully to the surface like flotsam and jetsam rising from a muddy bottom when the waters are stirred.

I see myself mirrored from head to toe in the revolving door of a grand hotel where the British Chess Championship, the most important tournament in the United Kingdom, is about to begin. We are in Ramsgate in the rainy summer of 1929. I am wearing a long tweed jacket, knickerbocker trousers that expose my scrawny calves, made even more noticeable by white stockings, and stiff, tight shoes, a real torture for someone like me who, until a few months before, was used to going barefoot. On my head is a white turban that towers above me by several inches at least. At my appearance I hear murmuring and some laughter in the room. I take a seat in front of the chessboard and hold out my hand to my opponent who pretends not to notice and, lighting a cigarette, blows smoke in my face. Nevertheless I smile. It is in my nature as a servant to always smile. Finally the long-awaited moment has arrived.

At Ramsgate, my detractors were lying in wait for me. After the mixed results I had gotten, everyone was curious to see how I would do. Furthermore, rumors were already circulating about the pending wager between the maharaja and the British Army major. The disparity of the stakes between the two bettors, two hundred pounds of gold against a miserable penny, was a detail that made the imagination gallop. Although not entirely confirmed, the unfounded report was spreading in chess circles. It was no small responsibility for me! Some, however, had already smelled a rat, sensing that this oriental-style blustering was hiding something else; they viewed me as a clearly propagandistic figure whose purpose was to draw the entire world's attention on India, for too long oppressed by British imperialism, and they conjectured that Sir Umar Khan's maneuver was none other than a symbolic attempt at revolt. Still today I have the strong suspicion that Sir Umar Khan used me as a pawn on the political chessboard. Already at that time, hotbeds of rebellion were cropping up throughout Punjab: the beginning of a struggle for independence that would only be resolved fifteen years later thanks to the peaceful revolution led by Mahatma Gandhi. But in those days certain thoughts never even occurred to me. I was completely wrapped up in the challenge that I would have to face.

As if the quintal of gold at stake were not enough, Sir Umar Khan wagered a large sum on my victory with a bookmaker. For my part I would have preferred not to know about it, since I did not yet feel completely confident. From time to time I still found myself confusing the Western rules and not taking full advantage of the possibilities in front of me.

I faced my first major tournament with a pounding heart. I felt that the outcome was entirely in my hands, but then again, in the face of any challenge, great responsibility calls for maximum concentration. Sir Umar Khan did not seem the least bit worried, on the contrary he appeared quite confident. It was not like him to lose a bet, and surely before making the wager he must have ascertained that the odds in his favor were convincing. His serene, optimistic attitude had a beneficial effect on me. In fact, as soon as I sat down in front of my first opponent, my fears vanished. It was as if every concern of mine had been wise enough to step aside, freeing my mind for the duration of the competition. After putting an end to the last game and sealing my victory, I had the feeling that I had settled a burdensome debt. I had to suffer a little longer to receive the official confirmation because, once the tournament was over, the commission met behind closed doors for more than an hour. It was the first time this had happened, and only later was it reported to me that during that period of time they had done everything possible to find some pretext to deny me first place. Since word had spread that I was not able to record the moves using the English system, all my game scores were scrupulously examined to find some error, an illegible move or a move completely unnoted. They went over the tournament regulations from top to bottom, looking for—and not finding—precedents that might justify a disqualification. Finally, late in the evening, the commission adjourned and the president came out, head lowered, to announce the name of the new champion of Great Britain in front of a waiting crowd of journalists. It had all gone so smoothly and turned out so well that the thought, immediately dismissed, even crossed my mind that the championship had been rigged, and that Sir Umar Khan had convinced Sir George Thomas and Frederick Yates not to participate in the competition. Or perhaps the palace astrologers, with whom he loved to surround himself, had predicted a sure victory for me. In any case, although there were many who did not recognize me as deserving, the victory was mine. Meanwhile Sir Umar Khan, besides winning the wager, had earned a nice little bundle by betting on me when all the bookmakers in the Kingdom gave me one to ten odds of losing.

I think that if Mälzel's famous automaton, nicknamed "The Turk," had returned to perform, he could not have been better represented. Dressed in European style, but wearing a tall white conical turban that contrasted with my complexion, making me look even darker than I was, I aroused enormous curiosity wherever I went. Naturally I was the favorite subject of photographers, who vied to portray me. Small and scrawny, I made a poor impression in group photos compared to the players of the time. I looked like an interloper who was there by accident, an amateur wanting to take advantage of the opportunity to be immortalized among the "greats." In me, there was absolutely nothing of that which I saw in the other champions: I was neither willful, nor cunning, much less elegant; I was just a poor Indian boy with a lost expression. How was it possible that this illiterate had so easily defeated all the British chess minds? And so the detractors took up the same old refrain, and the detested epithet of *idiot savant* appeared between the lines again, an expression that would plague me for life.

Moreover, it remained a mystery as to why the two best English players—Sir George Thomas and Frederick Yates—had abandoned Great Britain's traditional tournament. Was it fear of losing, or some kind of snobbery? Some journalists felt compelled to demand an explanation regarding the nature of their defection. And the excuses of the two champions, though not slow to arrive, were not very or not at all convincing. *The Times* directed a few pointed remarks at the two: "It was with great regret that all chess enthusiasts took note of the absence of the two most qualified British champions. Could they have wanted to postpone a confrontation with the Indian champion until next year, while for the moment merely studying his game? Physical indisposition and health issues make us suspect that a mysterious virus is infecting the best chess players in the United Kingdom, a virus that comes from the East and specifically from India."

Sir Umar Khan rewarded me by giving me a cobra leather belt, with a case containing twenty gold sovereigns, a sum that I would never have dared hope to have in my life. I immediately thought of my poor mother, and of how proud my father would have been, having taught me to play chess as a child. Finally my master was displaying the trust and gratitude that I deserved. At the same time, I had risen a few rungs in the domestic hierarchy and, although the distance remained unchanged vis-à-vis my master, I could now demand the services of the two servant brothers; it was a great satisfaction to see them polish my shoes and iron my shirts. Each time I beckoned they were required to come running without a word and bow before me while awaiting orders. There was no better balm for that black eye that still pained me.

In any case, two hundred pounds of gold taken from Sir Umar Khan's immense coffers would not have ruined him. Had he had as many as a hundred children from his legitimate wives, each of them would have inherited a patrimony surely greater than that of King George V himself. But for him, the fact of not only having won the bet, but of being able to trumpet it to the four winds and at the expense of poor Major Buchanan, was a satisfaction that had no price. Indeed it did not take long for this news to begin circulating among the journalists: news that no one had yet dared publish since it was uncorroborated. Sir Umar Khan did not miss the opportunity to humiliate his adversary. Right after my victory, during the press conference that followed, one of the reporters asked him whether his coming to Europe and my participation in the tournament were not, in fact, the result of a wager with a high-ranking officer of the British Army, and whether the stakes were actually a penny against two hundred pounds of gold. Whereupon Sir Umar Khan confirmed everything. This admission very quickly went around the world. As for Major Buchanan, he was not to be found anywhere in the United Kingdom, and nothing more was heard about the penny engraved with his personal dedication.

## 11

I must say that after a certain period of time spent in Europe, my vision of the game had become corrupted; it had lost the sacredness that characterized chaturanga. The magical aura that surrounded it had vanished entirely. Playing chess, checkers, backgammon, or any other game did not make much difference. Whereas in India a chaturanga master maintained a hieratic pose throughout the game, as if rapt in prayer or meditation, here they played without the slightest demeanor: the players fidgeted in their chairs, stood up to stand behind me, yawned, coughed, puffed pestilential cigar smoke in my face, drank whiskey, ate ham sandwiches and belched—perhaps imagining that I was Muslim and that the smell of pork would disturb my concentration. They dropped curls of ash on the chessboard and then blew them on me, or else they stared at me insistently just to make me uncomfortable. There was even one player who halfway through the game took out his glass eye and placed it casually beside the chessboard. What I perceived on the faces of my opponents, as soon as they found themselves in difficulty, was not surprise, but a kind of restrained contempt, a wary disbelief that presumed the execution of some diabolical trick on my part. Then, too, the fact that my stony face did not show the slightest emotion ended up irritating them: How dare I assume such an attitude of blatant arrogance? How was I able to endure every provocation with that perpetual little smirk on my lips? None of them bothered to conceal their hostility towards me. I could hardly accept such behavior, when in our country the opponent was sacred and had to be accommodated in every way. Indeed, my father had taught me that a game must be played on equal terms. To disturb the opponent's concentration was tantamount to cheating, and a victory obtained by improper means was spurious and unworthy, a stain that would weigh on the winner's conscience more than defeat would weigh on the loser's pride. Our religion teaches us that concealed behind every victory or defeat on the chessboard—and in life as well—lies the indelible design of karma: a victory can be a form of consolation, of encouragement, while a defeat can be read as an incitement or a warning. But, even knowing that everything has already been written, it would be a disaster to passively accept one's destiny; it would be a mistake to desist, to give up at the first difficulty, consoling ourselves with the thought that, after all, it's pointless to rebel ... We must apply ourselves to every undertaking as if our very life depended on the outcome of the game, because what matters is not the victory in and of itself, but rather the firm commitment we put into achieving it. What matters ultimately is what we accomplish ourselves, and it is only in this way that destiny can be changed while we are still alive. We can elude karma's design, because although it is true that it is already written, and therefore immutable, there is nonetheless the possibility of going outside its range of influence, of circumventing it, so to speak, by passing unnoticed. By changing oneself, one also changes the nature of one's atonement.

My career was meteoric, like the luminous trail of a Bengal light. It lasted for three years or so. It was an intolerable humiliation for my detractors to see me win the British Chess Championship again, twice in a row, and some found it embarrassing to have me captain the British team at the Olympics, but what left everyone stunned was the victory achieved in Hastings, in the match played against José Raúl Capablanca.

In your culture there is a saying according to which "clothes do not make the man." In India, instead, we are accustomed to the rule that clothing should correspond to the social status of the wearer. For us it is not possible to go unnoticed, to blend in with a featureless crowd; the colors of the garments we wear, the style of our headdress, and even the type of beard and mustache we have are expressly meant to set us apart and reveal the caste to which we belong. Consequently, finding myself in front of these European champions, my attention was drawn to their clothing, which very often—despite the person's acclaimed merits—was not unlike that of a common petty clerk. Seeing them sitting at the table, there was nothing that distinguished the champion titleholder from the lowest-ranked amateur. Often the jacket was rumpled, a few buttons hanging by a thread, the shirt collar had a greasy ring around it and the tie a very noticeable stain. There were some due exceptions. Which brings to mind the figure of Capablanca. I distinctly remember his well-groomed appearance: he was always impeccably dressed, and the edge of the handkerchief peeking out of his jacket pocket meticulously matched his simple tie, the knot attached to his collar by a silver pin. I can still recall his dark, somewhat protruding eyes and pomaded hair, the dry, vigorous handshake ... and that hint of lavender, something truly rare in an environment pervaded by a strong acidulous odor that was the very measure of the prevailing tension.

Everyone has always expected to hear me talk about the famous match in which I defeated the former world champion. Or at least to hear me talk about it with greater passion. The reason for my reticence was due in part to the limited mastery I had of the English language at the time, but also to the conviction that it was pointless to talk about it because words were ill-suited to the game. In this regard, I want to tell you about an episode that happened during the Hastings tournament. I was engaged in a game against Kmoch, who for the third time asked me to concede him a draw; when I didn't answer and just smiled, he jumped up from his chair and, looking around, said in a loud voice: "This is the third time I've asked him for a draw without getting an answer. What language does this fellow speak?" Whereupon Kishanlal Sarda, who acted as my second, approached to calm him down. "Sultan Khan," he said, "speaks only one language: that of chess."

Exasperated, Kmoch sat back down at the chessboard, and after a few moves the Austrian master had to surrender.

## 12

To return to the famous game against Capablanca: everyone imagines some kind of astounding report of a duel to the death. But it didn't happen that way. Perhaps it was a blessing to have no idea of my opponents' strength. What little I knew of each of them, I had heard personally from my master. For me, playing with Capablanca was no different from playing with Yates, with Alekhine, or with Tartakower. Moreover, one must never relax one's attention, neither with a master nor with the lowliest amateur. Kishanlal had the sagacity not to say too much about the strength of the adversary I was going to meet, and sometimes he kept me completely in the dark. Even today—assuming that there is anyone who remembers me—the victory over Capablanca is the first thing that my chess career is associated with; in fact it is the first thing that comes to mind when hearing my name mentioned. Although the match made me famous, nevertheless, taking into account all the defeats suffered at the hands of lower-level but by no means less aggressive players, that game turns out to be among my least brilliant. When I sat down in front of him, I did not know that until recently he had held the title of world champion. Only later on, analyzing with Kishanlal Sarda the best matches he had played, would I realize the finesse of his game. By this I do not mean to say that it was easy to beat him, far from it. I can only say that I was able to hold onto the advantage from the first to the last move, in a complex ending that screamed out for parity. Other than that, the game entered a phase typical of chaturanga which is called "the army in the quagmire." To win it I had to gather all my strength of mind. And only after exchanging my queen for his two rooks did I begin to see a possible glimmer of light. Keeping the queen, the only active piece of his game, in check was a long and patient effort. All the more so as the temptation to propose a draw, putting an end to the tension, intensified from moment to moment.

He would never have asked me for it, that much is certain: a former world champion would never stoop to propose a draw to a stranger, unless the parity were evident to even the lowliest amateur. And in this case I must acknowledge his probity; if he had asked me I would have conceded it without thinking twice, since I was at the end of my endurance. He had already spotted what for me would have been the winning maneuver, and he realized that it was useless to count on the possibility of leading me astray, snatching away parity through repetitious moves or by putting his king in stalemate. He was just waiting for me to make the move that he himself had already foreseen, and when I finally made the winning move, Capablanca smiled at me and overturned his king on the chessboard, without anger or envy, but setting it down softly as if putting it to sleep. Afterwards, commenting on the game, he did not hesitate to call me a genius.

I could say that this was the last important game for me. It is true that I played in Berne, in Hamburg, and that I won the British Championship twice more. Nevertheless, in some sense, a disconnection occurred. It was as if the wind had suddenly shifted direction. I found myself in a world that was not mine, and the very thought of being so far away from my homeland made me unsteady. Unlike Indian cities, where night and day people jam the streets by the thousands, London seemed to be inhabited by no more than a few hundred souls who roamed the dimly lit boulevards looking as if they had accidentally been locked out of their homes. The perpetually fog-shrouded city seemed to drift into a dream where each individual, even before appearing in the flesh, was preceded by his own ghost. Nights spent in the grand hotels were sleepless and fearsome, and the memory of my parents and the pain of losing them, so long suppressed, seemed to pour from my chest. It was not easy to get used to that environment. Something menacing hovered in the air, the harbingers of imminent catastrophe. I can say this today, but at the time it was just a disagreeable sensation. As war draws near, it is the world of art that is above all affected by it: the milieu that until then was consecrated to art—and I am talking about theaters, museums, exhibitions, expositions, spaces where enthusiasts love to gather—suddenly becomes the haunt of shady individuals. They do not have a name, they do not have a well-defined identity; they are wolves disguised as lambs that try in every way to win your trust, adopting well-proven techniques. They take advantage of the right moment to rescue you from a dangerous situation, a danger that they themselves have staged solely for your benefit, or better yet, solely for your harm. Agents. Informers! What else would you call them? I would come across many on my path. On the surface they are your friends, they know how to flatter you, they offer to help you, they advise you, they warn you, and then, in the end, they ask you for a small, very tiny favor in exchange for a big one they did for you. Did someone steal your wallet with all your documents? Well then they bend over backwards to find it for you. What would it take to return the favor by delivering an innocuous, sealed envelope in the next city you go to? A famous pianist will be performing tonight in London. Tomorrow, he will be in Paris, the day after tomorrow, in Milan ... Here is the ideal carrier to transmit a secret message: an old piano score to be delivered to a music professor, a score like many others, the only difference being that in this one, stuck between the notes, there is a microfilm no bigger than a semiquaver, and in that musical note there is a photo of a factory, the map of an urban area, of a military barracks, or a list of names. Simple pieces of information, similar to the tiles of a mosaic that will be patiently reconstructed. And the unaware messenger will not realize that just as he delivers the envelope, he will be immortalized by a passing photographer. And so, unbeknownst to him, our famous pianist will have become part of a criminal organization, it matters little which government it belongs to. He will simply be a pawn that can be exploited and sacrificed if necessary. This is just an example, of course, but there are other ways, ranging from sex, when it is outside legal sanction, to usury. Of course, the first step is the most difficult. Making contact with the subject and gaining his trust without arousing suspicion takes time, a long period of frequent association. And what is the ideal place to recruit someone? What more favorable terrain than an international chess tournament? Any stranger can enter the game room to watch the endless competitions, any player can be approached at the end of the game by fans asking for an autograph; dozens of photographers have unrestricted access, self-styled journalists cheerfully walk in waving a simple notepad. And in all that coming and going someone like me was constantly surrounded, either because of my successes, or because of where I came from. At that time, in fact, my country was under observation by the world press. By then it had become intolerant of foreign domination, though not yet strong enough to throw off the British yoke, and was therefore looking with interest at a possible ally: a certain German corporal who had already declared his intentions. As if it were a sign of destiny, the symbol that he had chosen for his flag was the swastika, which in India represents the sun, but whose display today is strictly forbidden throughout the world because of the evil that it is still able to evoke. As a public figure, I was in a difficult position: everyone wondered what I thought about the rebellious outbreaks that were taking place in my country. They asked me whether my victories on the chessboard were not a kind of symbolic revenge. And though the British press glossed over this aspect, the foreign press made the most of it. In India the advocate of independence, acclaimed by my people as a national hero, was the "condottiere" Subhas Chandra Bose, who was willing to ally even with the devil to finally free himself from British rule. And in the position I was in, I was exposed to all kinds of risks. Fortunately there was Kishanlal to watch over me, as well as the two "guardian angels" hired by the maharaja: "quick-change angels" I should have called them, given their ability to change their appearance and blend in among the crowd, becoming virtually invisible. I must confess, in fact, that I never spotted them, and only sensed their presence. The first time it was at Ramsgate, where a would-be journalist had begun pestering me. He asked me something that I couldn't understand. Perhaps thinking that I was pulling his leg, after a while he started to insult me—until two men arrived who, lifting him up bodily, carried him out of the hotel. The second time it happened at Folkestone, when the whole German Olympic team asked me to take a group photo with them. The photographer took a dozen or so shots, after which he gathered up his equipment and left the room. He returned shortly thereafter complaining that someone had attacked him, smashing his plates and exposing the negatives. Kishanlal Sarda, who had observed the scene impassively but who in his heart was grinning, warned me against allowing all the fly-by-night photographers to snap my picture, because a simple photo could be extremely compromising. Although

I may not have seen anything wrong with taking a souvenir photo with the German Olympic team, someone could read the wrong message into it, namely that I was inciting my compatriots to join forces with the German National Socialists. And since I captained the British team on the first chessboard, the allusion would become even more ambiguous. At that time I was not able to fully grasp the power of the printed word, and the significance of politics also remained somewhat obscure for me.

## 13

Ever since my country had begun to nurture clear sympathies for Germany's nascent National Socialism, rebelling more and more against the British Empire, people pointed at me on the street. Whereas, even well before then, I had never been met with widespread approval, I now found myself in danger of physical hostility, outright mob violence. Even in the most sumptuous restaurants—and perhaps it was precisely because I could afford them—the waiter served me my dishes with obvious contempt, and my hotel room would be carelessly made up, the housekeepers neglecting to change my washcloths and towels. I'm sure that every thirst-quenching drink I ordered contained the waiter's spit. Only a few months ago the newspapers had done nothing but talk about me, publishing full-page photos of me, and now everyone seemed to have forgotten. Yet up to that moment I had behaved in the most honorable way. Despite those who had questioned my abilities, I had won the British Chess Championship two more times, and in subsequent tournaments I had placed second and third behind outgoing and future world champions such as Alekhine, Capablanca, Euwe ... Although I had played successfully at the highest levels, my games no longer excited anyone. Even my victory over Capablanca was reduced to a simple bump in the road that the former world champion had experienced. I was a freak of nature, a curious phenomenon rather than a genuine chess master. As if to say: yes, he's good, but his skill depends on the fact that there's something wrong with his brain, an accident perhaps, a fall, a cerebral fever he had as a child ... and the appellation of *idiot savant* that I so dreaded recurred, as if I were an indelible stain on the history of chess, on the game where proficiency has always been associated with intelligence and the ability to reckon, but also with lineage. In *British Chess Magazine*, a group of psychologists wrote a brief essay on the extraordinary abilities of these natural geniuses, citing as examples several figures from painting, music, mathematics, and finally even chess. The authors were in agreement in concluding that all the individuals studied for their phenomenal mnemonic capacities, or for their prodigiously developed talent, had as their common denominator an IQ comparable to that of an idiot. Removed from their field—so they claimed—these individuals were like children, unable to provide for themselves, lacking any chance of surviving without someone's guidance. In the end they succeeded in making me despise the game that I had loved so much, to the point where I was ashamed of my victories and easily acceded to requests for a draw from some of my opponents, even when a win was within reach.

My chess career ended categorically and unexpectedly with the Folkestone Olympiad. I continued playing a few individual matches of secondary importance. Then, nothing more. By that time Sir Umar Khan no longer displayed the enthusiasm that had animated him in the beginning. It seemed that there were no more tournaments in all of Europe that wanted to invite me, yet I had played in the major competitions against players who were considered the best in the world. Nevertheless, the Federation no longer seemed to be aware of my existence.

The ensuing years were difficult ones: always following my master, who moved from one city to another, from one country to another ... I was often abandoned in a luxurious hotel for weeks on end. In the early days I could at least count on the presence of Kishanlal Sarda, but when he returned to India, where he had a family to look after, my loneliness became unbearable, magnified, moreover, by the constant, menacing sense of imminent war. I wondered what I would do if Sir Umar Khan never returned.

One day he called for me and for the first time he spoke to me like a son.

"Malik," he said to me, "I will have to leave for some time to get treatment. We will resume our plans when I return. I have therefore decided to entrust you to Lord Clearwater*, a great friend of mine. He is a kind, generous person and requires someone to look after Florence Hall, his country residence. The majordomo is of a certain age and is no longer able to run the house alone. Try to learn everything you can from him."

Thinking that my master's health problems would be resolved before too long, I decided to remain in Europe. Besides, there was no longer anyone waiting for me in India.

And so, I was entrusted to Lord Clearwater, who was none other than "the white hunter" who had accompanied the maharaja on the tiger hunt. I entered into his service at his residence in Surrey at the express request of the prince, who promised me that, as soon as he recovered his health, he

* A fictitious name adopted to maintain the privacy of an actual nobleman of the time [Note by Norman La Motta].

would return to enable me to continue my career. But something told me that I would never again resume playing chess.

## 14

I did not return to India, as some of my brief biographical mentions claim. I remained in England. My memory travels back to those places: I can still see the ghostly-looking villa rising in the midst of the misty English countryside. Lord Clearwater's residence was called Florence Hall even though it was the typical gray stone house, in the Tudor style, and there was nothing Florentine about it other than the lily depicted in the coat of arms above the entrance gate. And it was in Florence Hall that I spent the war years. At first I felt like an intruder. What I was doing there was not clear to anyone. Lord Clearwater had not yet given instructions regarding my presence, and I was left to settle in. The fact that my small room was in the

basement—the floor assigned to the servants—led me to think that I had become
part of the domestic help, even though no
one had yet told me anything, nor assigned
me the slightest task.

Lord Clearwater rarely showed up at the
villa, never stayed more than a day or two,
and seemed to be completely unaware of my
presence. During his absences, the staff
continued doing their jobs, but without
much enthusiasm. What my destiny would
be was a thought that tormented me day
and night. One morning, as though in response to my doubts, a letter was delivered
addressed to my name. In it was a deed of
transfer for an agricultural plot located in
Punjab: an endowment bestowed on me by
Sir Umar Khan. This meant, however, that
he was seriously ill, perhaps about to die,
and that I would never see him again. The
mere thought of no longer being under his
protection left me feeling anxious: I no longer had a role in life, I was no longer a chess
player nor a servant. And the surroundings
in which I was living were utterly hostile to
me. Even the domestics, who are usually so

assiduous about spelling out the internal hierarchy within their category—not to mention the distribution of duties, starting with the most humble tasks that were generally assigned to the newest arrival—acted towards me as if I were a low-ranking guest, some distant nephew of Mr. Charles, the majordomo, who had come to visit him, or a relative of the cook, if not the older brother of one of the maids. In fact, I ate in the kitchen but at a separate table, and I was completely ignored; no one ever spoke a word to me, except for the usual pleasantries. I realized that my presence was bothersome. So I started lending a hand with keeping the house in order. At first I chose to devote myself to gardening, helping a cantankerous old man who did not live at the villa but came from outside once or twice a week. The flowers and plants I cultivated represented the measure of time, the reckoning of the seasons, and finally of the years. They were the only hints of life, of creativity in a world that was always the same. And they had a therapeutic power over me. Deep down, I was still a servant of the land

and being close to it was like going back to one's mother to draw consolation from her. Still, there were also endless winters, and, had I not become friendly with the old majordomo, I would perhaps have begun to show the first symptoms of mental instability. Evidently Mr. Charles was in the same situation as I was. He did not have much in common with the cook and the maids. Being their superior, his job was to give them orders, and although there was a great age difference between the two of us, we were able to find at least a few common subjects. I tried to teach him to play chess, but it was a waste of time: his worst opponent, to whom he always ended up succumbing, was an irrepressible drowsiness, which interrupted every game at the start.

Mr. Charles must have been about sixty years old, and he was the prototype of the typical English butler. As with dogs that show their affection for their master to the point of resembling him, Mr. Charles had begun to take on the appearance of Lord Clearwater: the same receding hairline that exposed a bulging forehead, the same bushy scowl and mid-cheek side-whiskers, not to mention the hooked nose and white mustaches. He was shorter, however, by at least a few inches, and afflicted by a slight stutter. In that year of total inactivity, Mr. Charles saw in me not merely the one possible person to talk to, but a malleable element that he could mold in his own image. Having never married and having no children, he would have been glad to train anyone who might succeed him in the difficult charge of running Florence Hall. The English language was initially an obstacle, but in the end we managed to understand one another. And so he began to teach me the secrets of the trade: the arrangement of places at the table according to the guests' importance, the basic rules of etiquette, the timing between courses, the selection of wines, and so on. He then went on to reveal to me the villa's hidden architecture, with its network of secret corridors that, just by turning a knob or exerting the right pressure on a precise spot on the wall, allowed you to enter every room unseen. And finally he taught me how to drive. Mr. Charles had also been

Lord Clearwater's chauffeur, undertaking long trips, but his vision had considerably deteriorated in recent times, making his driving dangerous. There was therefore a need to find someone to replace him, and he thought he'd best teach me to drive the Rolls-Royce. Not only that, but he also explained all the functions of the engine, and the possible solutions in case of a breakdown—a very remote possibility, since the most important car manufacturer in the United Kingdom could boast of having never left a customer stranded on the road due to a malfunction, unless the car had run out of petrol.

In the short trips made in the surrounding district, Mr. Charles taught me to shift gears gently, how to take the curves well, and how to brake and restart without any jolting. The latter was a detail that would infuriate Lord Clearwater when he was a passenger, since he often utilized the time to take notes, using a tiny desk that the car was equipped with, and it didn't matter whether the road surface was smooth or riddled with potholes. As long as Mr. Charles was sitting beside me I had to obey his orders: I could not exceed the permitted speed limit by so much as a mile, and, although he might have sometimes seemed distracted, he perceived any slight acceleration in the engine. So, to satisfy my urge to drive the car at maximum power, I decided to take the car out by myself one day. I waited for Mr. Charles to retire for his usual afternoon nap. But I hadn't counted on the atmospheric quirks. Though the day had been predicted to be clear and serene, the weather suddenly worsened and fog rolled in, putting me in serious trouble. To avoid an overloaded hay wagon that had suddenly appeared in front of me, I ended up in a ditch. It took several men called to the rescue to get the car back on the road. Mr. Charles became very angry and for a while he didn't let me drive anymore, keeping his keys firmly in his pocket. Fortunately, the car had not even suffered a scratch. Weeks passed before Mr. Charles again let me drive, under his strict supervision, to the nearest village, where we had to go to get provisions, especially milk and powdered eggs, and the bacon that was much used. For the rest we had to make do with what nature offered us, that is, with the game on the estate. Neither Mr. Charles nor I had a knack for hunting. Mr. Charles, whose eyesight was getting weaker and weaker, had grown tired of firing his double-barreled shotgun right and left and missing, putting his own hounds in jeopardy of being shot. And I refused to take up a weapon because my religion forbade me. As a result, this typically masculine task fell to Miss Anderson, the sturdy cook, who, wearing mid-calf boots and a hunting jacket, would mount her bicycle and ride into the countryside with the shotgun slung over her shoulder, accompanied by two basset hounds who literally adored her. She would return after a few hours with a full game-bag.

During that year Mr. Charles taught me the rituals and rules of a perfect majordomo: with what I had learned, I would have been capable of running even Windsor Castle.

## 15

In early March, after a year's absence, Lord Clearwater announced his imminent arrival, throwing all the help into turmoil, since, lacking any motivation, they had meanwhile been carried along by inertia. Florence Hall abruptly returned to the real world. I still remember that moment clearly. The large dining room table was brimming with all the available silverware—that was the day to polish the cutlery in fact, a task reserved for the maids—and Mr. Charles was explaining the arrangement of those unwieldly, finely wrought utensils to me for the umpteenth time. I myself still hadn't quite gotten used to those contrivances that were employed to transfer food from the plate to the mouth, much preferring the use of wooden chopsticks. It was a Thursday morning, of that I can be sure, because that was the day of the week dedicated to general cleaning. For the occasion, all the villa's doors were thrown wide open, revealing, from the location where I was, a sequence of rooms that included the music room, the billiard room, the library, and, at the back, Lord Clearwater's personal study, which held a huge desk littered with papers spread out in wild disorder. Well, that's where the signal came from. From there the telephone rang after a year of absolute silence, a piercing sound that petrified us all, freezing us on the spot. Only Mr. Charles, immune to the spell it cast, began moving quickly, headed towards the source of that summons—namely, the nobleman's desk. After replacing the receiver he turned towards us, looked at each of us gravely, one by one, and, without any show of emotion, except for the sudden reappearance of his stutter, informed us that the master was returning.

Florence Hall seemed to awaken from a long lethargy. The good elderly Mr. Charles called upon the typical characteristics of the English butler—promptness, rigor, assiduousness—and that very evening he summoned us all to the music room. I immediately noticed that additional people had joined the serving staff: two twin sisters with a bewildered air, hired from some neighboring farm as reinforcements for the kitchen, and another middle-aged person, together with a young man who, given the marked resemblance, must have been his son, in charge of serving at the table. Mr. Charles gravely explained to us that from that moment on we had to be prepared to receive, with or without notice, an indefinite number of individuals who might well arrive at the villa in the middle of the night. Likewise, the pantry should always be abundantly stocked, to be able to meet the need to feed even an army. He informed us that in the following days a team of carpenters and woodworkers would arrive to make some modifications to the music room, instructing us to lend them our full cooperation. As for me, my job was to be the chauffeur. Mr. Charles was able to find a uniform in the wardrobe, perhaps worn by him some thirty years ago, that fit me perfectly, as well as a visored cap and a pair of driving glasses.

Two days later the team of carpenters arrived in a van. First, they unloaded a few rolls of wallpaper in the courtyard, and finally a table disassembled into several pieces that seemed more suited to a ministry's conference room than an aristocratic residence. All those things were brought into the music room. The door was locked and the renovation work began; that's what it was called by Mr. Charles, who, observant of his master's orders, did not concern himself in the least about what was taking place inside that room. At other times, his spirit of preservation, rightly befitting a major-domo serving for over thirty years in the same house, would have been alarmed at the mere sight of a hammer; the mere idea of having to drive a nail into a wall to hang a painting on it would have sent him out of his mind. Instead, I saw him walk by the door, calm and serene, despite the horrible racket that came from it. Rather than a renovation, it sounded more like a thorough demolition. In short, the music room was emptied of every piece of furniture and the table that was over forty feet long was set up in the center of the space. That was what I managed to glimpse before the door was finally shut once and for all, as soon as the work was finished, with a sign forbidding entry hung on the knob.

While we waited for the master's arrival, Mr. Charles and I occasionally got into the Rolls to scour the English countryside in search of provisions. None of us knew whether Lord Clearwater would show up at the villa alone or with guests. In any case, we had to be ready for any eventuality. The pantry was now jam-packed with anything you could wish for, an abundance of tea and coffee had been bought on the black market, and the cook had resumed her full authoritative standing. Instead of the usual stew at meal-times she served us new recipes, demanding that we give her a dispassionate judgment.

One day a telegram arrived announcing

Lord Clearwater's arrival the following day at noon, with a request to go and pick him up in London.

By now the United Kingdom had entered the war. At the train station, military-troop trains left the city, packed to the hilt, with scores of girls in tears to see them off. Every house displayed its flag, and walls were covered with posters urging young men to defend their homeland. His Excellency was not at all surprised to see me driving the car, in fact, he even seemed pleased—a sign that he wasn't too confident in Mr. Charles's vision and reflexes. For my part I did my best to make the trip comfortable for him, such that it enabled him to pull out the tiny desk set into the arm of the seat, and make notes in his notebook. That was the acid test, after which, having passed it, I was tacitly assigned, in Lord Clearwater's presence, and with Mr. Charles's blessing, the role of chauffeur. An important duty, because I was the only one who, night and day, could ensure a connection between the villa and the rest of the world. Once this role was handed over to me, I felt buoyed up: I had a specific assignment. The responsibility of being issued a Rolls-Royce exceeded the simple job of driver. It wasn't enough to wipe a damp cloth over the windshield and chassis. The cleaning had to be thorough, every single bolt had to be polished, and the same care had to be given to the engine which, with its marvelous, orderly tangle of brass tubes, resembled a portable pipe organ. Mr. Charles himself, in complimenting me on that field promotion, could not conceal his emotion, announcing in advance that, starting the following month, I would even receive an appropriate compensation. He added that I should not have any illusions about loafing around the rest of the time, however, because there was always a lot of work to be done at the villa.

Lord Clearwater acted as if he had only been gone a few days. He skipped lunch, to the cook's immense displeasure, and shut himself up in his study, ordering only a ham sandwich and a glass of warm milk for dinner. The following morning we drove him back to the station in time to catch the train for Liverpool. Before getting out of the car, I heard him instructing Mr. Charles to look after it, since it was "an extremely rare piece of merchandise." On the drive back, I tried to question Mr. Charles about what the merchandise was, but he actually didn't know either.

## 16

Over the next several days vans from various shipping firms began to arrive at Florence Hall. Workers unloaded wooden crates, no larger than a medium-sized trunk, but apparently extremely heavy, as they were brought into the house with special lift trolleys. I myself had tried to move one, but I had not been able to budge it one millimeter, almost as if it were glued to the ground. I wondered what they could contain, certainly something valuable, judging by the care that Lord Clearwater demanded of the staff responsible for the unloading. These items came from companies all over Europe: El Viejo Dragón in Barcelona, Country King in Scotland, Esposito in Naples, Montanari in Florence ... One day a bill of lading came into my hands that read *Metal Models.* Yes, but models of what? Crates of this kind continued to arrive, to be deposited in the music room in the custody of Mr. Charles, who each time, following the delivery, locked the door properly, attaching the usual sign to the handle. Meanwhile, however, I had managed to take a peek at the room and the changes that had been made in the interim. To begin with, all the chairs had been moved elsewhere, with only a few left against the wall. The oval table, at least forty feet long and twenty feet wide, was enthroned in the center of the room. The total lack of chairs around the table suggested that one would be able to move around it freely. Bonded to the tabletop was an extremely detailed world map in relief: a true masterpiece of cartography.

We all wondered what was going on in that room. The fact that it had been locked, forbidding us access, only intensified our curiosity; the content of those crates in particular was cause for much discussion among the servants. That was all they talked about. Some claimed that it had to do with

England's entry into the war after the occupation of Poland by the Nazis. Surely it was ammunition, or maybe weapons, and in all likelihood Florence Hall was about to become an arms depot. This did not explain the presence of the gigantic planisphere, however. Others maintained that, given their weight, those crates contained gold ingots, a government gold reserve intended to be used for the construction of heavy weaponry. One day a team of men in overalls showed up, armed with crowbars that would have been the envy of a crew of burglars. They went into the room making sure to close the door securely behind them. For an entire afternoon, until late in the evening, we heard the typical creaking sounds made by boards being unnailed one by one. After which the team left, carrying away the empty crates and packing material, and leaving the mystery of their contents intact.

## 17

What could be so secret in that room that it had to be kept locked, hidden from the servants' prying eyes? A servant is not a person like any other; although he is capable of performing certain tasks, he is not very unlike a statue. He has no feelings, no will of his own, no ability to discern or to choose, nor is he allowed to know anything beyond that which is countenanced by his master. In the presence of a servant the master feels he can behave with the same freedom that he would permit himself in front of his dog. In actuality, it's not that he trusts his subordinate's discretion: he's well aware that the servant listens and remembers, and that at the first opportunity he will report what he has heard to others, since it is in his nature to gossip. But the master also knows that it will all remain confined to the circle of domestics. The bond of discretion elevates the servant and, to some small degree, relates him to nobility. So I wondered what was so precious in that room that he had to hide it even from the eyes of his most trusted retainer.

It was not long until, driven by curiosity, I decided to take a look at the music room, or at what was left of it. And it was on that occasion that Mr. Charles's teachings proved useful, enabling me to enter the room without having to force the lock. As you may have guessed, it was not a matter of passing through walls, or resorting to picks, but more simply of using the secret passage that ran behind the main walls and that, in this case—if I remembered Mr. Charles's instructions well—would lead to an opening near a massive pendulum wall clock. The route started from the basement. Only the majordomo, being the sole person to have access to the wine reserve, was aware of it. The entry was through an ordinary door, hidden behind a shelf of empty bottles. From there you had to go up a wooden staircase and slip into a corridor, or better yet, into a hollow space that, due to the sagging walls, had become so narrow in some places that you had to suck in your breath in order to pass through. It was certainly not ideal for those who suffered from claustrophobia, which explained why Mr. Charles had never wanted to take me through it in person, merely showing me the layout with a drawing. Failing to find a working flashlight, I had resorted to an oil lamp, and as I moved cautiously, I was assailed by the most catastrophic thoughts, in the worst of which I pictured Florence Hall burned down in a fire caused by the oil lantern slipping out of my hand. If I remembered the instructions well, the opening that would take me into the music room should be marked by some Roman numerals on the wall.

It may well have been decades since that passage had last been used; it took everything I had to move the massive wall clock, behind which the opening was hidden. The music room was dark, lit only by the oil lamp I held in my hand. I took a few steps, trying not to make a sound. I knew very well that there was no one in that room; nevertheless, a specific behavior corresponds to every act of transgression, and that of walking on tiptoes, as I was doing at that moment, was the movement of a thief, or at least of someone illegally entering someone else's house. I was conscious of the violation, but my curiosity was greater. And as I took step after step, holding my breath, a mirror reflected my image covered from head to toe with white filaments of cobwebs. I looked like someone awakened from the dead, who had just emerged from a crypt. I thought of the face Mr. Charles would have pulled if he had caught me in that state. I looked around, and saw a diffuse greenish glow rising from below; it seemed as if the floor, all around the huge table, had been polished with an opalescent liquid, but I couldn't make out what it was—until the light of the oil lamp revealed a sight that I would never have thought to see in my life. So this explained what the "metal models" meant: they were tin soldiers, models of warriors with their relative uniforms, as well as ancient war machines, elephants, boats, horses, on up to cannons, tanks, and aircraft of the most recent era. There were thousands of them, arranged in orderly fashion: a sight never before seen, never imagined, not even in the most daring depictions in the *Mahabharata*.

The reason for such secrecy only became clear to me later on. Lord Clearwater, like a skilled set designer, had wanted to hide the work in progress to present the finished result to the public when it was fully complete. After a week, in fact, he returned with some people, a dozen in all, for whom twelve rooms were readied. These individuals, including our master, closed themselves in the music room each day to "work." Of the entire serving staff I alone knew about the "work" that was taking place in there, and I was careful not to reveal that these staid gentlemen, all elderly, and some very old, in their improbable uniforms, were nothing more than overgrown children, engaged with solemn graveness in playing with lead soldiers.

Until the day of the inauguration arrived.

A festive day to which even the weather contributed, giving us several hours of sunshine. However—and I say this parenthetically—the full light only emphasized the villa's flaws due to the passing of the years: stained walls, peeling plaster, dusty windows ... But never mind, by now I was looking at things with the critical eye of an aspiring majordomo. It was actually a memorable day in which about thirty invited guests came from outside, a party that opened with a sumptuous lunch, which Miss Anderson had put her heart and soul into preparing. A lunch that, thanks in part to the fine wines, inspired people to sing patriotic songs. Finally, before cutting the ribbon and entering the music room, or rather, the game room, Lord Clearwater himself gave a short speech about the organization's goals. "The Masters of War" was the name of this cultural association that had found its permanent home at Florence Hall. Its members came from different countries, and until then had set out to strategically analyze the great battles of history on whose outcomes humanity's destinies had depended. Now they had the rare opportunity of being able to play along by analogy, tracing a world war that was fully underway. For these pugnacious combatants in miniature, Florence Hall became a real battlefield or, as you Westerners say, the microcosm, the convex mirror of the material world, the source of all prime causes. It became a citadel, a refuge, a laboratory, but also a place you were not allowed to leave without due permission. Today they talked of El Alamein, tomorrow about Stalingrad. Meanwhile, London was being systematically bombed. Swarms of planes obscured the sky, and cluster bombs passed over our heads, headed for railway junctions, bridges, and connecting roads. Some exploded in the surrounding countryside, but the objective was clearly elsewhere. In those years the war industries worked at full capacity. At times there was great ferment around the planisphere followed by whole days of inactivity, when time was measured by the ominous tolling of Radio London that, from time to time, dispatched its encrypted messages over the air. From morning until late at night those individuals took turns around the table, moving armies with the same dexterity with which a roulette habitué moves his chips on the green carpet. All at the command of a general who, with a long croupier's rake, directed operations. Naturally I was fascinated each time I paused to follow the game. It was just like watching the progression of a giant game of chaturanga. What difference was there between the infantry and the deployment of pawns? Or between tanks and chariots? Or the horses and the light artillery? And even if there were open spaces instead of square boxes, mountains and rivers, hills and ravines, it was still a chess board. A game, therefore, albeit more complex, but still a game, guided by the same rules of war on the battlefield. And just as if I were watching a game at the table, I didn't always find myself agreeing with the strategy chosen by the player whose turn it was. In fact, one day when I had entered the room pushing the liquor cart, I noticed that there was an unusual silence around the table. I stopped to watch. The situation was intricate, difficult for both sides. They were all sure that the result would be an outcome with neither winners nor losers. For a moment I forgot where I was and what my duties were, concentrating on finding a solution. The players did not like having one of the servants observe them while they were engaged in their strategies, and at that moment I was caught in the act. The man who reprimanded me was the general of the day, a choleric little man, with purplish wattles, whom I had several times heard animatedly discussing the progress of some military operation with his colleagues.

"Hey, you, why don't you pour us a drink rather than just standing there gawking and poking your nose into business that doesn't concern you?"

His words roused me, bringing me back to this world, but not without having snatched the solution from the gods. Unexpectedly, Lord Clearwater intervened in my defense: "Why don't we hear what our chaturanga expert thinks?" And then, looking around and seeing a big question mark on everyone's face, he hastened to explain everything. After revealing to those present that I was a formidable chess player, and three times British champion, he concluded by saying that I was also an expert in the oldest war game in the world, the chaturanga in fact, and anyone who knew this game extremely well could predict the outcomes of any battle. This last assertion was greeted with universal laughter. Even I was taken aback. It was really unusual for a Westerner to know this rule from a very ancient decalogue, but perhaps Sir Umar Khan had spoken to him about it. "Well then," the choleric general interposed, "let's see him prove it to us." With no hesitation, I gave them my answer: one of the two armies should retreat and leave the battlefield, which for the most part consisted of swamp lands, capable of causing all the heavy vehicles to get stuck. Whoever strategically retreated first would have the victory in hand. This prognostication of mine was received with the benefit of the doubt, but after a few days, when Radio London confirmed my predictions down to the last detail, I suddenly became part of the circle.

**18**

Today, with hindsight, the conditions in which the Western world found itself can be exhaustively analyzed. But for me, at the time, it was like groping my way through the fog of the English countryside. Operation Ikarus, Operation Kathleen, Operation Barbarossa ... the names designating the various military actions underway meant nothing to me, nor could I convince myself that elsewhere, far away, thousands of miles off, certain battles were actually being fought by living human beings, leaving behind a sea of blood. And it never occurred to me that the whole world was fighting an enemy that had no qualms about trampling on every decent value, leaving millions and millions of victims. For me, the military formations that were moved on that gigantic planisphere had no specific connotation, they were simply characterized by their different colors: red, white, and black soldiers, and lastly blue ones, just like in the chaturanga. Consequently my responses were not at all biased.

In order to make you understand how my expertise in the game was exploited, I must explain how my mind worked, before it completely lost its powers.

You Occidentals almost always completely distort our philosophy. An example of this is the Master's maxim which says: "Sit on the bank of the river and wait to see the corpse of your enemy pass by," words that are often interpreted as a kind of incitement to revenge—a deleterious emotion that you in the West compare to a dish that is best served cold. For us, instead, the meaning is quite different: our enemy is the mind, and we must block the flow of the mind, stop the association of ideas, if we want to ascend to a higher level of consciousness. As the Master says: "He who (erroneously) thinks that he himself is the subject of the action is still the slave of Maya; he who knows Reality on the other hand knows that he is only a spectator."

It is not easy for a Western mind to imagine how it is possible to choose absolute passivity, or non-action, just when the most critical action is called for. And this was precisely the tactic I often adopted in the game, detaching myself from conscious thought, and waiting for the *atman* to appear, the multiple-form being that is within us, who would show me which piece to play. This, of course, did not happen with every move, the request had to be urgent and come from my soul, like an actual matter of life or death. Then the god Ganesha would appear, the elephant-headed child with a broken tusk—symbol of the denial of the duality of thought—who would show me the right move or the winning strategy.

The infallibility of my responses earned me the preeminent position of "adjudicator." I was consulted at every dispute to give my authoritative perspective.

Nobody was aware of it, but among the members of this society there was what you

Westerners call a "mole," that is, a spy, ready to take advantage of any suggestion that could prove useful to the enemy. Lord Clearwater may have been the only one who smelled a rat, noting an extraordinary correspondence between the game and actuality: indeed, curiously abrupt strategic reversals took place on the real battlefield, very similar to our moves. It was hard to believe that they were mere coincidences, but I am still reluctant to think that I might have been the deus ex machina of the situation. At that time I was so impressionable that often I couldn't help wondering if Florence Hall wasn't the place where humanity's destinies were being decided. I could never imagine, however, that I had become an instrument in the hands of a secret agent, who was now so convinced of the accuracy of my predictions as to make them his own and convey them to his covert superiors as ascertained facts. Thanks to me, one of those men was garnering endorsement to merit a future decoration. Maybe an Iron Cross.

A rather widespread maxim among you Occidentals is that a butterfly flapping its wings can trigger a hurricane a great distance away: just one way of affirming the existence of a connection that links all phenomena occurring in our world. It is more difficult to believe that the fluttering of air by a butterfly's wings can make the fury of a hurricane subside, or that an immense, inexorable catastrophe can be stopped, or diverted, by a simple word. Nevertheless, it may be that a single grain of sand in the gears can slow down or stop the most powerful machinery. I can believe, therefore, that at the most decisive moment of that war—when the two opposing forces were in a state of stasis due to perfect equilibrium, such that the weight of a fly would have sufficed to nudge the scale's needle and thereby determine the fateful supremacy of one of the two sides—my opinion was taken as the response of an infallible oracle. Even today I like to think that at a critical juncture, where misinformation and misdirection were no less important arms than the most deadly military weaponry, my wrong advice helped save the world.

This is how it happened. When it came to the crucial point of the conflict, and the awaited landing of the allied troops in Europe, transported by amphibious craft, I was asked where the invasion would take place. As I had done until then, I tried to concentrate on waiting for an answer. But it did not come to me. No matter how hard I tried, I felt only emptiness and silence, as if it were a unanimous denial by the gods. So in the end I made my own decision, relying on the fact that the odds were always fifty-fifty and that even if I were wrong I would not cause any harm. I pointed my finger at Calais, confirming that the landing would take place there. The date, incidentally, was June 5, 1944. Contrary to my prediction, the Allies landed the following day on the coasts of Normandy.

After I had pronounced my response, there were several minutes of disconcerted confusion. The general, skillfully maneuvering his croupier's rake, moved the allied army into the indicated area. All eyes were fixed on the map, on that point in Europe where the event was to take place, when suddenly our attention was drawn to a noise coming from the courtyard: it was a car engine. We all rushed to the bow window, just in time to see the car speed out through the gate. It was the Bentley that belonged to a Belgian man, a docile individual with thick glasses and a collar beard. Monsieur Dupré, I believe he was called, and it certainly had never even crossed my mind that he might be a secret agent of the enemy forces. It occurred to me, however, that I had caught him standing by his car one evening, talking to someone who seemed to be sitting in the back seat. As I passed by, though, I was surprised to see that there was no one inside the car, nor anywhere around. At that moment, however, I didn't think anything of it, judging the practice of speaking aloud to oneself a widespread senile habit. Only later would I learn that a two-way radio in perfect working order had been found, until then well hidden in the trunk of his Bentley, abandoned in the middle of the fields.

The undercover agent had managed to get away, thinking he had obtained the most valuable piece of information. By now, the last act having been concluded, the theater could be destroyed along with all of its puppets. In fact, not more than two hours after the mole's escape, a German plane flew over Florence Hall dropping bombs that hit the main body of the villa, reducing it to a pile of rubble.

I woke up in a hospital bed, plastered from head to toe, with fractured arms and legs and a concussion that had caused me to lose my memory. It took months and prolonged exercising to regain the use of my limbs. And my memory as well, over time, was able to piece together one fragment after another. But when I began to take my first steps without anyone's help, I realized that I was under close surveillance. That was when the first interrogations began.

## 19

Conflicts never entirely end: they reappear under different, unsuspected guises. In the future, the theaters of war will no longer be those of land and sea, or of sea and sky, but of the human mind. Weapons will become increasingly sophisticated, no longer made of metal, but often residing in the brains of rare individuals who, though unaware of their powers, will be able to decipher any cryptograms capable of reading other men's minds—and not only that, but of swaying them to act in accordance with their will. They will have the power to predict events and even modify them. Psychiatrists and psychologists, shamans of the mind, are well aware that man is already undergoing a transmutation, whose results will begin to be clear in the near future, but whose progress can be accelerated by studying the brains of those individuals with singular mental abilities and powers. And I, seemingly, was one of them, one of the many subjects to be studied. Hypnotism, thought transmission, telekinesis, prescience—all faculties common to gurus and yogis—had for some time been subjects of study for the scientists of the unnamed parapsychology society in whose care I was. Evidently, many had been aware of my extraordinary faculties of prediction even before the bombs destroyed Florence Hall. Equally evident was the fact that "The Masters of War" society had not been formed for the sole purpose of playing games. The discovery of my faculties had made me the guinea pig ready to be dissected on the anatomical table of science. For as long as it was possible, I hid behind the excuse of amnesia. However, these people became more and more insistent. They began making veiled accusations towards me, followed by equally veiled threats, and when I was fully recovered they moved me to a psychiatric hospital where

I was subjected to a series of electroshock treatments which, almost certainly, caused the loss of all my mental faculties. I managed to escape from the clinic, stealing a car from one of the psychiatrists. Fortunately, I still had my belt with the twenty gold sovereigns given to me by Sir Umar Khan, some of which I used to pay for my voyage on a Norwegian whaling ship that made a stop in New York after a good three months of sailing.

And that's how I landed in an unfamiliar metropolis, with false documents in my pocket. Fortunately it was easy to keep a low profile, given the state of great confusion that reigned in New York. My first job was at the Barnum circus, reduced to being a stable boy and looking after a dozen elephants, but after a short time I was fired because of my spirited protests over the cruel training techniques adopted by the so-called tamers ... Those electrical jabs that were widely used, even on newborn elephants, reminded me of the electroshocks that I'd undergone in the psychiatric clinic. After leaving the circus, I found refuge in the Indian community, which had already claimed several areas of the city, opening shops for spices, carpets, and precious fabrics. Short in stature, dark-skinned, my fellow countrymen would constantly gather in small groups to chatter on street corners. In actuality they kept watch over the territory, ready to sound the alarm as soon as they spotted a police car. They reminded me of ibises, birds sacred to some, but certainly not attractive specimens. I did not forget, however, that the same blood flowed in my veins.

In addition to selling, Indians and Pakistanis—always vying with each other—had cornered the taxi monopoly. At the time there were several car rental cooperatives that sliced up the city of New York like a cake. One of them, the NY Cab Corporation, the company I started working for, had taken the biggest wedge. It was a grueling job, but the only one I could risk taking, unless I wanted to be a dishwasher in some disreputable Chinese restaurant. I was hired with no hesitation because, besides knowing how to drive any car, I had some notions of mechanics—indispensable given the fact that many of the cars were held together by paint. First of all, with the help of a street map, I had to memorize the city, or at least the island of Manhattan, where the taxi was the form of transportation most used by people who didn't have a minute to spare. For us Orientals, haste is not a priority, and therefore, fearing that our philosophical indolence might negatively affect receipts, courses had been set up that we were all obliged to attend, on pain of dismissal. Of course, these classes took place a couple of times a month during our free time and we were not paid to be there. I, too, was one of the instructors. I taught the raw beginners the basic principles of how an internal combustion engine works. Often, in fact, when a car broke down, it didn't take much to get it moving again, even if just to bring it back to the garage. The most frequent problem, however, was always that of running out of gas. Another instructor, a gigantic Sikh with a fearful aspect, taught us how to avoid danger. To begin with, he told us how to defend ourselves against ill-intentioned characters and drunks, who were capable of making off with an entire day's earnings just to be able to afford a last quick drink. The job was not without risk, especially for those who drove night shifts. Despite precautions, however, accidents occurred regularly: in the last month alone one of my colleagues had his car set on fire, and another ended up in the hospital after a shootout between the police and a robber who had commandeered the taxi as a getaway car, threatening to shoot the driver if he so much as took his foot off the accelerator. The vehicle had crashed through a shop window and both men had come out of it with contusions.

Every Monday we were given a schedule, to be updated as needed, which listed street closures due to work in progress, flooding, or marches and demonstrations. One might think that the city's traffic would be to the taxi driver's advantage: the longer it took, the longer the meter ran. But it didn't work that way, because when a customer ended up stuck in traffic, he left the driver a nickel or two and continued his trip on foot. We had to get by somehow: pay for an insurance policy out of our own pocket, maintain the car assigned to us, and assume responsibility for any eventual harm to ourselves and to third parties. What with one deduction after another, we were left with only a few dollars, and to survive we had only the customers' generosity to count on: in effect, any real earnings came from tips. So it was essential to take good care of the passenger and try to anticipate his needs. In the end, if treated well, the customer would be favorably disposed and would open his wallet with a broad smile. All this could only be learned through experience. Being able to identify the most open-handed, generous person in a waiting crowd was not easy, just as it was not easy to hit it off by exchanging a few words along the way; it required a particular sensibility. Many of my workmates knew only a word or two of English and sometimes preferred to remain silent during the ride. I, on the other hand, made an effort to communicate. After my stay in England in the service of Lord Clearwater, something of the pretentious ways that distinguished the serving staff had rubbed off on me, and although I was not thoroughly proficient in the language, I was able to recite certain polite phrases quite well.

## 20

It was on a day in late July, driving down Fifth Avenue, that I came upon Mrs. Abbott. She was sitting on a suitcase waving her cane whenever she heard a car approaching. My first impulse was to pass her up. At the time I tried to avoid elderly people. They were too demanding, too troublesome, and, besides, they still had not understood that the value of money was the most unstable thing in the world. For them, a dollar was still a dollar. Try and tell them that in the meantime there had been a world war that had resulted in inflation and a progressive increase in prices. The tips they bestowed, therefore, were still those of the pre-war period. And this white-haired lady, waiting for a taxi, was certainly in her eighties. So, as soon as I spotted her, I stepped on the accelerator. Immediately afterwards, however, I was seized with remorse for having left that poor woman to roast under the July sun. I felt a strange sensation: a kind of inner imperative that told me to go back. I hit the brakes and peered into the rearview mirror, hoping that one of my colleagues had meanwhile picked her up, but the woman was still there, sitting on her luggage, holding up her cane. I backed up, stored her things in the car, and helped her get in. I estimated that she must weigh not more than ninety pounds, a weight that, given her height, made her as slim and elegant as a reed. I avoided asking her why she was in that part of the city. It must surely have been the result of an argument with a taxi driver. Many of my coworkers, in fact, were extremely touchy, and if someone merely questioned their choice of route, that person was likely to be dumped in the middle of the street.

"Young man, the Plaza!" she ordered me, poking my shoulder with her Malacca cane. From her tone of voice I could tell that she was a woman used to commanding. I realized that she was blind, not only because she wore large dark glasses, but also by the cane that was painted white. The fact that the lady wanted to be taken to the most renowned, and also the most expensive, hotel in the city left me puzzled. And to think that I had a whole list of comfortable, moderately priced hotels in my pocket, from which I collected a percentage for each new customer I brought in. But she had shown such confidence in choosing that one, that I did not think I should step in. I simply took her to her destination, with the utmost regard for her age, avoiding bumps or abruptly stepping on the brake, just as I would have transported a precious crystal chandelier.

When I pulled up in front of the Plaza, the uniformed doorman, complete with an admiral's bicorn hat, ran to open the door, bowing profusely, and a few minutes later the reception-desk clerks also came out into the street. Judging by how they received her, Mrs. Abbott seemed to be at home in that hotel. And here I had mistaken her for a pauper! After paying the fare and leaving me a princely tip, Mrs. Abbott handed me her visiting card. She asked for my address in return, and since all I had in my pocket were a few brochures with the NY Cab Corporation's phone number, I gave her one of those with my name written in pencil at the bottom.

It wasn't until a few days later, leafing through an old magazine, that I discovered by pure chance that "the poor old woman" whom I had picked up in the street as an act of charity was in sixth place on a list compiled by *Vogue* recording the ten wealthiest women in America. There was also a photograph of her, taken at least twenty years ago, where she was all dressed in white, wearing a broad-brimmed hat, going up the steps of a private twin-engine plane on the arm of a man who must have been her first husband. The article referred to the Abbott family, magnates of the iron and steel industry, who had made all their foundries available for manufacturing heavy weaponry during the war. I found some additional information in *Who's Who*: after being widowed, Cecilia Abbott had married a second time, to a surgeon associated with a humanitarian organization; she had moved to India, to follow her husband, and had remained there until her spouse's premature death. Despite her age, she was still to all effects at the helm of Abbott Industries.

Something told me that I would be meeting her again. Faith in karma makes us see everything in its dual aspect: the first, invisible, has already happened, like the whistle of a locomotive that precedes the train's arrival; the second, about to happen, is none other than its material replica, the train traveling at a rate that deviates to a greater or lesser degree from the sound signal. In the place where Parvati sits on her throne, the encounter with Mrs. Abbott was already present in the warp and weft of her garment, woven with colored silks and golden threads. The rest was yet to happen.

**21**

A couple of weeks later, when I had already forgotten this episode, I was summoned by my boss. Except for the day I was hired, it was the first time I was asked into his office. I immediately thought that I would be reprimanded for some failing. Perhaps some passenger had been unhappy about how he had been treated. Sometimes one of us would be wrongly accused or suspected. So as I climbed the stairs, I could feel my legs shaking.

"Sit down, Malik," the boss said. He turned his back to me and flipped through the drawers of the employee file cabinet. "Ah, here's your folder!" The fact that he had not yet looked at me made me fear the worst. He leafed through the file that concerned me, lingering over a few points, and finally a satisfied expression passed over his face. "I see, Malik, that so far your performance has been good."

"I do my best, sir."

"Mrs. Abbott phoned yesterday asking for you." And when I didn't answer, he added: "Mrs. Abbott. Does the name mean anything to you?"

I pretended not to remember. "Oh, was that Mrs. Abbott? Yes, I think so. She asked me where she could contact me and I gave her the garage number."

"She wants to take a long ride to New Jersey with her car, which hasn't been driven in years. And she wants you as her driver. No one but you. Can you drive a Rolls? Hey, Malik, I'm talking to you!"

The boss's thunderous voice woke me from my brief daydream. His big bearded face was just a few inches from mine. He was sniffing my breath to see if I had been drinking.

"Are you sleeping, by chance? I asked you if you can drive a Rolls."

"Of course I can drive a Rolls," I replied,

somewhat piqued. "In London I was in the service of Lord Clearwater for years. And if I know something about mechanics today, it's because I studied the engine of a Rolls from top to bottom."

"You know who Mrs. Abbott is, don't you?"

"I am well aware."

"Get dressed up. And be on time. Hey, Malik ..."

"Yes, sir?"

"You haven't started seducing old ladies, have you?"

The next morning I took extreme care with my appearance, put on my livery and cap, and headed to the Plaza early enough to make sure I was on time. When I got to the hotel I found a surprise waiting: parked in front of the entrance was a Rolls-Royce Silver Dawn. Mrs. Abbott was already waiting for me, sitting in the back seat. Although it was a quarter of an hour before our appointment, she seemed impatient. I left my taxi in the care of the doorman and hurried over. With my new uniform, cap, and goggles, I really looked good in that Rolls. I wondered what my coworkers would have said.

During the day we toured all of her properties in New Jersey. She spoke with the overseers, asked about the yield of the harvests, about the health of the livestock ... She even insisted on riding a horse, and there was no way to make her change her mind. Later she reassured me by saying that she had not been in any danger because the horse she had mounted was Dolly, the most gentle mare in all creation. Lastly we stopped near an old stone house, the place where she had spent her childhood.

There, Mrs. Abbott moved from room to room, pausing to sniff the air or run her fingertips over certain curios. She asked me to describe the subject of the paintings and their location. She lingered for a long time beside a window as if listening to a distant voice.

On the return trip, throughout the ride, the lady's manner towards me changed: she did nothing but bombard me with questions to which I replied promptly, not concealing anything from her. I described my stay in Europe in the service of Sir Umar Khan, and then Lord Clearwater, I even told her about fleeing to America to escape the parapsychology society, which British counterespionage was behind. I told her about the years I spent in New York, about the difficulties I had to overcome each day ...

Only at the end, when we were already approaching the Plaza, did she ask me to enter into service at her home. She said that the apartment would be ready within a week and that she needed someone to be with her to assist her with small, everyday matters; for the rest there was the domestic help, from the cook to the cleaning lady.

I had served Sir Umar Khan, and Lord Clearwater, not to mention that as a taxi driver I had been providing my assistance to unknown passengers for months, and now this lady was once again asking for my services. Was it really my destiny to be a servant? At the moment I did not know what to answer. The first thing I thought to ask was whether the contract provided for a weekly day off. Mrs. Abbott laughed: "All the time you want," she said.

Realizing that I had perhaps asked an inappropriate question, I tried to offer the excuse that every Thursday I went to the Manhattan Chess Club. In reality, I had never set foot in the prestigious New York club. I had tried once, but I had been refused, perhaps because of my dark skin, or perhaps because I did not have a letter of introduction. Since then I knew better than to try again, and if I ever felt like playing chess, I went to Washington Square Park, when the weather permitted, where it was not difficult to find some opponent itching to put himself to the test. Other than that, I had no friends, and no wife either. In India, unlike in the West, love stories between strangers do not happen. Marriages are arranged by negotiation between the elderly members of two families who have known and respected each other for many years. Everything is conducted as a simple business transaction, unbeknownst to the interested parties, who most often have not even reached adolescence. And of course the two spouses, whether they are children or adults, must belong to the same caste. At forty years of age, getting married according to tradition becomes impossible, especially living abroad. I often envied my coworkers who lived in a real house, where there was a wife and children waiting for them every night. For a while I had enjoyed the warmth of a home with an Indian family from my own village, who had sublet to me, at a reasonable price, a room without windows, scarcely larger than a closet, which barely held a single bed. Their children, two school-age boys, became fond of me and called me Uncle Sultan. But with the arrival of a third child I was forced to return to the dormitory owned by the company I worked for, which was located above the taxi garage. The big rooms were cold in winter and sweltering in summer, with half a dozen beds, all occupied by castaways like me.

On the one hand, Mrs. Abbott's offer was tempting; on the other, it seemed "all too tempting." I wondered why on earth, with all the unemployed Indians who were running around New York, she had chosen me, a middle-aged man, not at all attractive, with not much education. Then I did a thorough assessment of the situation I was in: at the end of the war Sir Umar Khan had died and I had been left without anyone to rely on. It is true that he had left me a plot of land in the Punjab, but a single person was not enough to work it. Moreover, I did not feel like going back to be a farmer, so I had ceded the land to my uncles, with the clause of repossessing it if I were ever to return. I was in my forties, I was penniless, forced to earn my bread day to day. As if that weren't enough, the diagnosis of the last doctor who had examined me was not encouraging: discovering shadows in my lungs he had recommended a richer diet and, possibly, healthier air. Finally, the suspicion that I might have colluded with the enemy during the war—an accusation liable to years in prison—along with the idea that I might have special psychic powers that allowed me to foresee events both weighed on me. In either case I would serve my sentence behind four walls for the rest of my life.

It took a week before I found the courage to knock on her door. In such a luxurious building, in midtown New York, you cannot enter as if it were just anywhere. The concierge desk is a real barrier, a counter bursting with telephones and intercoms, staffed by an individual who must surely be a former policeman. A shabbily dressed man, what's more with dark skin, is not well received in certain milieus, and if he appears a little too insistent he will find himself face-to-face with internal security or the neighborhood cops. I had to be extremely cautious, because if the immigration officials found me, I would be sent back to India immediately. I told the concierge that the lady was expecting me for an urgent job. I also showed Mrs. Abbott's visiting card, which functioned as a clearance pass. Before letting me through, the Cerberus made a phone call to make sure I was telling the truth. The elevator took me to the top floor, into the interior of the penthouse. The fragrance that hovered in the rooms, so different from the usual smell of fried food and grilled meat that permeated every neighborhood of the city, brought me back to my early childhood and I had to contain a surge of emotion. I found myself in a sumptuous apartment, tastefully, though somewhat simply, furnished. Mrs. Abbott was waiting for me, sitting in a large wicker chair with her Persian cat curled up on her lap. She took off her glasses, exposing a face that, although covered with wrinkles, still retained its very fine features. The wandering blankness of her gaze confirmed her blindness.

"Come here, come closer," she said in an inviting tone. She reached her timeworn hands towards my face; she touched my forehead, ran her forefinger down the midline of my face, lingered along the curve of the nose, and finally she brushed my lips with her fingertips. In her way she was satisfied. She asked me to accompany her to the roof garden, which required going up a spiral staircase. Walking through the apartment with her holding on to my arm and at the same time guiding me, I had a chance to look around. Precious carpets hung on the walls, while the floor itself was bare. A necessary precaution in her case, since she was at that stage of life in which everything conspires against the body's safety. Slipping in the bathtub, like tripping over a rug, could be fatal to her. The spiral staircase led out to the terrace. But the term *terrace* is, if anything, restrictive, since what we entered was a huge greenhouse, a glass bubble, literally another world. I found myself in one of the many gardens that adorn the temples dedicated to our divinities. Whoever designed it could only be a master Indian gardener, the combinations of the various species attested to it: maritime pines, sweet gum, and red maples. There were small waterways crossed by little wooden bridges, fountains, pools with water lilies and gold fish; spaces covered with very fine sand, with smooth boulders of slate and black marble. Along the path, among ferns and mosses, there were places of meditation and small votive temples dedicated to Hindu gods. Mrs. Abbott explained to me that not a drop of rainwater was wasted, since it was collected in a large cistern and conveyed to an autoclave that fed the waterways as well as a capillary irrigation system. Even in times of drought not a leaf turned yellow.

So I finally accepted, and indeed, as had happened to me in the past with Sir Umar Khan, I had once again risen from the dust to enter a gilded world.

The years spent with Mrs. Abbott represented a period of gained awareness, years of maturation. Because Maharani was an "old soul": a person who, after having lived many lives, had overcome illusory reality and was now approaching the last existence before being liberated from *samsara*, the yoke of deaths and rebirths. There was more devotion in her little finger than in my entire being. Evidently even our meeting had been willed by karma, since each of us needed the other: she to complete her journey, I to begin mine. That was where the word *marriage* became twisted, misunderstood by everyone. Ours was a spiritual marriage, but no one wanted to understand that, least of all (and he pointed his finger at me) your fellow journalists, who continued to accuse me of defrauding her, persuading her to marry me so I could get my hands on her fortune. What would I have done with all that money? You tell me. How would I have managed it? It would have been taken from me in no time, in one way or another. And in any case, my karma would have been affected. No one was able to understand that there was a strong attraction between our two souls, even though I felt that, compared to her, I was still very far from reaching the destination.

Maharani was my master, my mentor, my mother, my bride, my spiritual guide. It was she who gave me an education, who transformed the poor *carnac* into a moderately cultured person. Sir Umar Khan, while appreciating my talent, had never concerned himself with my education. On the contrary, if only he could have, he would have displayed me in the guise of the "boy adopted by the apes." Since he had taken me to Europe to put my skill to the test, such proficiency would have appeared even more extraordinary in an uncouth illiterate, barely able to express himself. Besides, no one demanded a higher education from a servant; on the contrary, at the time we arrived in Europe I embodied the ideal figure of the noble savage, domesticated by the white man—a caricature emphasized even by the cinema, a cliché aimed at spreading certain dangerous racial theories.

Maharani, on the other hand, wanted to shatter this barrier and began by teaching me to read and write in English, attending to my diction in particular. She said that my pronunciation was as grating as a fingernail scraped on a chalkboard. She reasoned that it was better to pronounce a single word correctly than to garble the contents of an entire dictionary. The lessons lasted no less than two hours each and took place daily at the same time, from four to six in the afternoon. I simply had to read the page of some book aloud to her, repeating it until I saw that she was satisfied. Of course, by reading and re-reading the same pages many times over, I was also drawn to the content, to the point of wanting to know more. In that way, besides improving my diction, she was able to instill in me a curiosity for certain topics that we would later study together. The first times were really difficult since I had to grapple with a language that I had always hated; I would never have agreed to do it if it hadn't been she who asked me. It took a few years to achieve acceptable results. In the end, however, I too was pleased. Not just for the way I expressed myself, but for all the notions of general culture that she managed to impart to me, without my ever getting bored. I realized then that knowledge can be a key to freeing ourselves from the chains of illusion. She found reason to teach in everything: it could be the title of a book, the poster for a film, or, when we were driving around Manhattan, a statue or a building. This made me think that, given certain conditions of lighting, she could still see just enough to distinguish one object from another. In any case, Maharani never missed an opportunity to teach me something new.

In return, she never demanded much from me. It is true that from time to time I cooked for her, but only because I was a repository of several exotic recipes that probably no one in all of New York was able to make successfully. To see to the household there was a stream of other people: a masseur, a doctor, a hairdresser, a dressmaker, a cleaning lady ... even a cook who prepared meals under my supervision. Moreover, Maharani ate like a little bird and would very often leave her food untouched on the plate. She had become—and was increasingly becoming—an ethereal, spiritual being. She would have me do a few small errands, but I would be lying if I said that she took advantage of me.

It took some time to get to know all her qualities, and to realize that in actuality all the events of my life, some happy, some tragic, had led up to this encounter. Maharani had sensed from the very first moment that she could place her complete trust in me. And now I found myself being her guardian and her guide. She had lost her sight due to the trachoma she contracted during her stay in India. Despite her disability, she was a woman of great vitality. She did not like to stay shut up indoors, especially in fine weather. And any excuse was good enough to go out. Often, I had to accompany her to make purchases. She took me to the tailor to have some new clothes made for me. We went to Broadway on every opening night. She loved to invite people to the house, mostly painters, musicians ... She financed a fledgling orchestra, she was a patron, especially of painting. She liked to help young artists: she would buy one of their paintings and then exhibit it in some prestigious art gallery, convincing a famous critic to write about it. When she learned that I did not know even one of the great masters of figurative art, for a whole week she had me take her to the Guggenheim to teach me the whole history of painting through the works on display. She knew the layout of the museum in detail, and the location of the works. She remembered the paintings perfectly, not just the most famous ones, and was able to describe them down to the smallest particulars. Of course, there is a notable difference between Western pictorial art and Eastern painting. The latter remains bound to mythical or religious canons, while the former, instead, claims absolute freedom of expression. I often found it difficult, in fact, to understand the reason for certain transgressions against the harmony of nature, and some of the questions I asked myself then, as a man completely devoid of culture, have not found a convincing answer even now that Maharani has made me a reasonably acculturated individual.

Some might think that the mood at Maharani's home was heavy and serious, but that was not the case. She often asked me to plan cocktail parties, which were then followed by weeks of meditation and prayer. These quiet little parties, at which artists chatted until the wee hours, were sometimes attended by famous musicians with their bands. Seeing them arrive was always a surprise. They came from Harlem, from clubs like the Lenox Lounge and the 55 Bar. They would come by when it was already nearing dawn, just to have "one last drink for the road," and you could predict the outcome of their visit by the fact that they had brought their instruments with them, even the huge double basses that could barely fit in the elevator. And, lo and behold, ready for the occasion behind a revolving wall was a Steinway concert grand piano. Performing were authentic jazz legends: John Coltrane, Charlie Parker, and, one evening, even Duke Ellington. When I told Maharani that their names meant nothing to me—good heavens!—she hastened to take remedial action, as she had done earlier with regard to painting. Mrs. Abbott owned at least a thousand records on which to base an actual lesson plan, which had me listening to music from morning till night.

But the best memories are the trips we took with the car. I think I must have driven tens of thousands of miles and visited the most important cities in North America. Already in early spring she liked to leave the city behind and be ferried around the countryside.

There was one place that Maharani loved especially. We often took the Rolls and drove out to Long Island, where she had a wood-shakes cottage, painted blue, overlooking the ocean: the perfect place for a quiet picnic on the beach. Of course we counted on a nearby village of fishermen who had known Mrs. Abbott for many years and who were willing to offer us fish caught before our very eyes.

Even today, I wonder how I could define myself in terms of my role with Mrs. Abbott. I might be able to arrive at it through a process of elimination, as I had done with the first policeman who, right after her death, questioned me about my presence in that house. I remember that it was a rather awkward situation for him, an interrogation that had its comical aspects. To the direct question of whether I were a relative, I replied no, I was not.

"And what are you doing in this house?"

"I live here."

"Do you pay a regular rent?"

"I am not a tenant."

"So you are a servant?"

"To call myself a 'servant' I would have to have been hired, have a health insurance card, and a specific job, but my duties, if I can call them that, were of a diverse nature, and ranged from driving the car to preparing certain cream desserts that Maharani loved."

"And who would Maharani be?"

"Mrs. Abbott, of course."

The policeman, a heavyset man who was

short-winded and had a bronchial whistle, stared at me as though he suspected I was pulling his leg. Just looking at him made me feel like laughing, but I restrained myself out of respect for the deceased. Despite every effort on my part, he did not seem convinced: I did not belong in that house, I could very well be a thief, and I might even have caused the lady's death myself.

Apart from her blindness, Maharani certainly had a sturdier constitution than mine. Only in recent times had she begun to turn inward. Until then she had shown great interest in life. A great desire to teach, but also to learn. She wanted me to explain chaturanga to her at all costs. Chess was not enough for her. She had even ordered an antique board of painted wood. She had it sent directly from India, and it must have cost her quite a lot. To satisfy her I took on that task, although it was difficult—not just because of the complexity of the game, but also because her condition did not allow her to even see the board, let alone distinguish one piece from another.

But she was not discouraged. She maintained that everything that reaches consciousness passes through the mind even before it reaches the eyes. For that matter, I was never able to really understand how much she did not see. A blind person, when he talks to you, cannot focus his eyes on yours, he glances over them. She, instead, looked you straight in the eye, making you doubly uncomfortable. Perhaps she had periods when, thanks to the medication she regularly took, her vision experienced some improvement; still, I am inclined to believe that at times, especially in front of a stranger, she would exaggerate her incapacity in order to gain a margin of advantage. Or perhaps her blindness was getting worse. It is possible that she realized that the glimmer of light, that small peephole on reality, was slowly but surely closing completely. Or maybe it was her age that began to weigh on her, I don't know. In reality she suffered from heart problems; I had realized that from the bottle of nitroglycerin she always kept at hand, a medicine that Sir Umar Khan also used. The fact is that in the last months she had completely lost her verve. She spent more and more time in bed. At those times she would ask me to read aloud some pages from the *Vedanta* or the *Bhagavad Gita*. But she tired very quickly and fell asleep. The flame of those sainted words had died out, only the warmth of the ashes remained. The serene atmosphere that had reigned in that house for so many years had changed. The executor of her will came more and more often to have her sign mountains of documents. She herself gave me an envelope to be opened only after her death. I did as she wished. In addition to a letter, there was a document transferring title to the Rolls-Royce. I kept that letter, and I read it so many times that by now I know it by heart, word for word. But I would like you to read it for yourself.

•

Sultan Khan went to rummage in his cabinet and shortly afterwards handed me a sheet of paper that had been folded and refolded so many times that it was now crisscrossed by an indelible web of creases.

Dear Malik,

When you read these words of mine, I will be gone. I have arranged things so that no one can make any claims against you over what I have left you as a token of my gratitude and in full possession of my mental faculties: first, a small monthly sum, which will be paid to you by my lawyer. It will serve as a means of support for you and also for Asha and Gangesh, whom I hope you will look after. The apartment, in fact, will remain yours in usufruct as long as you comply with this simple charge. Asha is over twenty years old and she does not have much longer to live"—in fact, I found the cat stiff on her pillow two weeks later—"but Gangesh is still young. Among other things, he belongs to a very long-lived species of parrots, and it is possible that he will outlive you. For all routine and extraordinary expenses related to the household, contact Shuster & Bros. who have your file at hand. I did not want to leave you money, of which I consider myself only the custodian; instead, I make you a gift with a light heart of the Rolls that I inherited from my father, and that I consider entirely mine, a means that you will require if you should ever decide to return to your previous job. With the cap and goggles you can afford to take on only upper-class, wealthy clients. Do not take my offer to continue living in this house as a constraint: know that you are free to leave whenever you wish, because I have already given instructions, should you decide not to stay, for someone else to look after my animals. I would prefer you to do it, but don't feel obligated in any way. Asha, wild as she is, will not give you great satisfaction. Gangesh, on the other hand, needs a lot of affection. Attend to him, let him talk ... who knows, one fine morning his voice may become a melodious song. If that should ever happen, it would be a sign that They are already here and that a new era, less appalling than the one we live in, is about to begin.

"They? Whom was she referring to?" I asked.

•

With those last words, Maharani was referring to a legend of uncertain origin, according to which, at the dawn of Creation, the Gandharvas, celestial musicians and song masters, supposedly existed. The task of these winged beings was to teach all birds to sing. But since many birds, though splendid in their plumage, had been left with a grating voice, and some utterly mute, the master singers were to return to complete their mission. The legend is still handed down and disseminated today by some tribes of Nepalese nomads, who make a living going from village to village where, for a few rupees, they offer theatrical representations of this ancient belief. In their performances they announce the coming of the song masters, whose advent will be preceded by a profound silence that will mark the end of Kali Yuga and the beginning of a new "golden age." Their arrival is hailed as a blessing. The members of this tribe wear splendid garments adorned with multicolored feathers, and, accompanied by their long flutes, they sing melodies never before heard. They accept food, hospitality for a night, and the donation of a few rupees. Finally, they continue on their way, leaving their mark in the song of the local birds who, hearing that music, learn new modulations of their natural register. Maharani and I often joked about it, wondering if it would ever be possible for silence to reign over New York for even one thousandth of a second. Not to mention the night she passed away, which had been particularly earsplitting: a raging storm, in fact, had struck Manhattan and must have caused fires in Queens, because for several hours I heard ambulances and fire engines heading in that direction.

I should have realized right away that Maharani was dead by the fact that she hadn't called me, as she always did when bad weather was on the way, to ask me to please make sure the shutters were closed tight. Instead of approaching on tiptoe as I often did to check that she was breathing, I had only peeked into her bedroom: protected by the veil of mosquito netting, the motionless figure of her body, stretched out under the sheet, had assured me that she was deeply asleep. Still, the strange behavior of Gangesh, the parrot, should have already alerted me. It is well known that there are sensitive creatures, capable of detecting their master's state of health and even of sensing his imminent death. And that night the bird was particularly agitated: he kept pacing back and forth along the bar of the perch, dragging a stiff, half-open, seemingly broken wing, and emitting shrill cries. It looked as if he himself were wounded and about to breathe his last. I thought he was frightened because of the storm, but instead he was mimicking the death of his mistress. The cat had gone into hiding, the parrot seemed crazed, and the only one who had not yet realized that Maharani was dead was me. In truth, I could not accept the possibility that such a perfect world could end in the blink of an eye.

## 22

Everything that followed the discovery of her death was shelved in a corner of my mind, like a fact that did not concern me. All I remember is that faced with the duties I had to attend to, starting with notifying the children of their mother's death, I was seized by panic, and at the first light of dawn I telephoned Mrs. Abbott's lawyer, asking him to come to my aid.

I must say that I admired the way the corpse was transported with the help of a wheelchair by four solemn women in tailleur who, having closed ranks around the lifeless body, practically glided out of the room. Not a word about her funeral, observed strictly privately, was leaked to the press, except after the ceremony had taken place. I know for certain that Maharani wanted her body to be cremated, but I am equally well aware that her last wishes were disregarded and that she now lies in the family tomb in Connecticut.

After her death I should have collected my thoughts in prayer, but it is not easy to do so when there is a pack of jackals in double-breasted suits around the house, sent by the court. I could not have objected to that intrusion, even if I'd wanted to, because they all had a legal permit signed by some compliant judge. In the days following Maharani's passing, the most bizarre individuals streamed through the house. It seemed they all had a passe-partout that allowed them to come and go as they pleased. Starting with the police and private detectives who tried to intimidate me with the oddest questions. Then there was a swarm of lawyers, ready to defend me for mind-boggling fees; fortunately, however, Maharani had already entrusted my case to one of the most renowned law firms in the city.

The intruders started with an inventory:

half a dozen people, their attire and expressions contrite, invaded the apartment to do an accounting and appraisal of every item. And in that house I myself was considered little more than a curio among the many that at that moment were being inventoried. From time to time a voice rose, reeling off: "Letter opener with an onyx handle and a pinchbeck metal blade of modern manufacture"; or: "Old-fashioned bronze incense brazier with a border adorned with bas-reliefs depicting Indian divinities; jacaranda wood tray ..." There was one official who dictated aloud to a second official, while a third one checked that what the first reported to the second corresponded to the truth. Finally, a fourth official checked everything again and made sure that every object was returned to its exact place, within the mark left in the veil of dust that had settled on the furniture during those days. Even my closet was inspected with meticulous attention, including my underwear. What aroused their curiosity most of all were those long strips of white muslin that, draped at the waist, formed the typical dhoti pants—

worn long down to the ankles or knotted at the waistline—that were paired with a short jacket buttoned up to the neck: at-home attire, suitable for everyday and every season. But there was also a series of Kiton and Rubinacci custom-made suits, to be worn at the theater or on important social occasions. Obviously, those were my personal belongings, but try telling them that! They went around the house from morning till night with large notepads in hand. Every so often someone would pause to observe me, perhaps tempted to add me to the list. What would he have written in those notes? Object of dubious provenance? About five feet tall? Dark-skinned? Approximate age: fifty? I wondered how long I would have to put up with their presence. With the furniture and fixtures they had an easy time, but when the time came to catalog the entire library, title by title, author by author, and the dates of publication, it would be another matter; I estimated that it would take a week or maybe two before they completed their work.

The animals did not tolerate them well either: the Persian cat, after Mrs. Abbott's death, had holed up somewhere, while the parrot observed the intruders and their movements with great interest, trying to imitate them. One man in particular had been targeted: a little fellow—to be clear, smaller than me—with thick glasses, who examined each object with a magnifying glass. As he brought his head close to the object, with one eye closed and the other wide open, he looked so comical that it made an impression on the parrot. The bird, doggedly trying to imitate him, would tilt his head to one side, wink one eye, then give vent to all his vexation by raising shrill, ear-splitting shrieks.

Finally, there were the tax agents. My presence in that house was considered suspect, or at least irregular. I lived in the house, but I was not a relative; I had domestic duties, but I received no salary except in the form of *argent de poche*. I was therefore in the lady's service, though I did not have a document attesting to it, and was found to be propertyless, despite the fact that I was wearing custom-made clothes. Could it be a clever way to evade taxes? Perhaps among the many definitions I could have suggested to them was that I was simply a friend. Meanwhile, the tabloid press was digging through my past. Not to mention all the heavy-handed allusions regarding our prolonged cohabitation under one roof.

The legitimate heirs did not concede easily. I was dragged into court several times. The signed, handwritten letter by which Maharani gave me the precious Rolls was subjected to several calligraphic appraisals. And, of course, the inquisitors wanted to know what my previous job had been.

I merely told them that in England, for the duration of the war, I had been the assistant majordomo at Florence Hall, the residence of a Lord, and that later, after moving to New York in the early postwar years, I had been a taxi driver for some time, along with dozens of other Indians and Pakistanis. I omitted the fact that before that I had worked in the hell of a Chinese kitchen, that I had been a newsboy on the streets of Manhattan, or the sandwich-board man for an Italian pizzeria. Above all I kept silent about the reasons that had driven me to leave Lon-

don and embark on a Norwegian whaler
that had nearly shipwrecked near the Baffin
Strait ...

•

"In the end, however, you won the case," I said.

"I won the case, thanks to the letter that I had
you read, which was recognized as authentic."

"Nevertheless, shortly after Mrs. Abbott's death
you left the apartment. Why?"

"It was because of Gangesh's suicide."

"The parrot?"

"That's right. After Maharani died, Gangesh
sank into a state of severe depression. He yanked
his feathers out one by one, and became completely unrecognizable. The veterinarian told me
that he was suffering from loneliness and that
perhaps I should find him a companion. But any
attempt to provide him with a female of his species was in vain. And one day when I let him out
of his cage in the apartment, he disappeared
through a window that had been left open. I
couldn't catch him in time. Frantically flapping
his wings, he tried to fly as high as he could, after
which he drew in his wings and let himself fall

from fifteen floors up, smashing onto the pavement below. That tragic episode led me to leave the apartment. I sold the Rolls-Royce for a tenth of its value and returned to India."

Sultan Khan remained silent, but I could see that there was still something left unsaid.

I tried to encourage him.

"Is there anything I can do for you?"

"Should there ever be any proceeds from the publication of my memoirs, I would like them to be donated to the mission. As you can see, there are numerous repairs to be made."

"I will not fail to do so."

"I have still another favor to ask of you."

"Anything."

"I would like to ask you for a free subscription to the *Post*."

You had only to look around to see that the Comboni mission was certainly not the most suitable place to have the morning paper brought to you on your breakfast tray. The cost of a daily paper would be enough to feed a sick person for at least two days. In that refuge for castaways they lived isolated from the rest of the world. The few news items that came from outside were either reported by word of mouth or read in scraps of the crumpled newspaper that was used to pack fruit, to keep it from being bruised during transport. Months-old news, sometimes years old ... this paper was collected before it went to be pulped, and you were fortunate to find any recent news in it. In a corner of the room was a pile of pages torn from various publications, among them the *Post*. It was clear that they had been carefully ironed out one by one, then pressed under the weight of dozens of old telephone directories. Sultan Khan must keep them so he can read them at his leisure. Realizing that my attention was drawn to them, he tried to excuse himself.

"As you can see, there are not many newspapers around here: we are always quite a bit behind with what is happening outside. Unfortunately you can never read a complete news article. It looks like war with Pakistan is about to break out. But don't ask me who will come out the victor. Perhaps because of the electric shocks I underwent, certain faculties were lost to me some time ago, and any prediction of mine could result in a grave blunder. And you, in America, what is happening there? Is it true that man will soon go to the moon?"

"It would seem so."

"And what do they say about that fellow, a certain Fischer who is trouncing the greatest Soviet champions?"

I hadn't told him, but I was no longer the chess enthusiast I had been as a youth. I followed the story, more than anything else, because of its political implications concerning relations between the United States and the Soviet Union.

"I think he's very good," I said.

Sultan Khan's eyes lit up: "Good? To me, he is a genius. I have followed some of his games and I can say with confidence that he will become the world champion. The person who will have to beat him to hold onto the scepter will have quite a responsibility on his shoulders."

I took advantage of his fervor to ask Sultan Khan if he had any regrets.

"There are two things I am sorry I did not do," he answered. "The first concerns my betrothed."

"Your betrothed?" This was news to me.

"Yes. Earlier I had been assigned a wife. We had never seen each other, but someone had decided for us. Having lost my parents, Sir Umar Khan himself chose the woman with whom I was to share my life. Her name was Dayita and she was a year younger than me. She had a privileged position in the servant hierarchy. She was in fact a lady's companion, whose job it was to brighten her mistress's life. Therefore she had to be able to read and write and be well educated. And in addition, Dayita could also play chess. After the wedding she would enter into service at Sir Umar Khan's home. Everything was arranged, and upon my return from Europe there was to have been a ceremony to consecrate our lives to forming a family. But unfortunately she died before we had a chance to meet. She drowned, swept away by the engulfing river that flooded our village. I often wondered if I could have saved her. An idle question, since hypotheticals are pointless when they refer to the past. In the end, after returning to my country, I married a very distant cousin, a widow, with four already-grown children. I left her the land that my benefactor Sir Umar Khan had given me. I married her to give her children a less difficult future, but right after the marriage she revealed herself for what she really was: a cunning, shrewish woman, who did everything she could to make my life hell, to the point that I was forced to leave home. I found refuge in this mission to which I donated all the remaining money that I had set aside. A year ago, my condition worsened: the illness that had lurked silently in me for so many years suddenly erupted and I don't know if they will be able to contain it this time."

He paused before continuing.

"The second regret has to do with the game. I was born to be a servant, and this talent for chess did nothing but deprive me of the humility and rigor required by my caste. The splash of brilliance that was given to me at birth is similar to a drop of wine that can single-handedly pollute an entire well of pure water. I never considered myself a great player, because mine was a natural gift. It wasn't I who devised or conceived of strategies, I merely waited for the genius governing the game to suggest the right move to me. Being supported by the gods is not as great a thing as everyone believes after all; acting while dangling from their strings, becoming their pawn, is not a distinction. It is little more than a servant does when he obeys the wishes and commands of his master. The nickname *idiot savant* foisted on me scornfully by a losing player haunted me all my life, but it also opened my eyes: what we manage to construct laboriously on this earth counts much more than what is handed to us from the heavens. Nevertheless, my talent left behind a legacy of vanity that still causes me pain over a glaring injustice. When the International Federation coined the official title of Grand Master for the first time, it was deservedly conferred on many, but no one remembered my name. No one expressed any sort of judgment on my game, no one took the trouble to analyze my matches; only Raúl Capablanca, who was certainly not gentle in his assessments, recognized my genius. All the others looked the other way, as if I didn't exist."

An attendant entered, pushing a cart with a large pot of steaming broth. He set the table for Sultan Khan with a tin plate and plastic cutlery. A ladle of soup, a crust of bread, and a piece of foil-wrapped cheese were his only supper. I was politely asked to leave.

Before going, I inquired if he needed any medications. He asked me to send him some vials of streptomycin, the only remedy for his illness.

"And don't forget a subscription to the *Post* for the mission."

Those were his last words.

## 23

When I left the mission it was already evening. An interminable column of trucks crammed with soldiers was passing through the village, raising a cloud of dust that, in the last light of day, took on a violet hue. For a moment I thought I had come out on the wrong side of the building, because all the stalls that had livened up the area when I arrived had now disappeared; likewise the din raised by dozens of clamoring children chasing about had fallen silent. There was no one on the street anymore, only the persistent rumble of the truck convoy, which seemed neverending. Through the flapping edges of the tarpaulins, soldiers in camouflage could be glimpsed, helmets on their heads, rifles planted between their knees, sitting in double rows on rigid benches, facing one another, as if seated at a rustic table. I waited for the last truck to pass before heading for the jeep that I had left in the shade of a gigantic banyan. I barely recognized the vehicle under the couple of inches of dust that now covered it after countless transport columns had passed by. The sun was setting, and although it was still bright, it was a suspended luminosity in which shadows were lurking and which would not last long. From one moment to the next darkness would fall and erase everything with a single stroke. I wanted nothing more than to leave quickly, but the strangest thoughts were popping into my head. Would I find my way home? Had I checked the engine's oil? And the air pressure of the spare tire? What if the car broke down along the way? The area I was in was considered a war zone, and I could inadvertently trespass and run the risk of being killed. And all of a sudden a swarm of children of all ages came towards me, their hands outstretched in an unmistakable gesture. Someone once told me that in India you should not have a soft heart, and that you should never give children money if you don't want to interfere with their karma and suffer the consequences. A suggestion that was ignored: I did not do it because I was driven by compassion, but only to be rid of their noisy intrusion. I dug out everything I had in my pockets—a handful of coins which, added together, would not have even bought me a glass of water—and scattered them on the ground. There was a real scuffle, then each of them vanished with the miserable treasure he had managed to scrape up. Only one boy had not moved from his place and he stood there, motionless, both arms holding a basket of sorts, made of woven straw. For a moment I thought he wanted to sell me something, maybe some mangoes that he had picked himself. I regretted not having anything left in my pockets to give him. But when I was a few steps from him, a shiver ran through me from head to toe. It was not a child! He may have been fifteen or sixteen, maybe even older. His stature was due to the fact that both his legs were amputated at the knee, and he was able to stand by resting his armpits on a pair of short wooden crutches. I immediately knew, from the amputated legs and bandaged hands, that he was a leper, cared for at the Comboni mission for who knows how many years. I had seen cases like that before: orphaned children, segregated, kept hidden by the family's shame, forced to share a cramped space with work animals, barely fed enough to remain alive; creatures who have been denied any form of learning, including speech, abandoned in a sub-human world made up of corporal needs and raw emotions. One might wonder who had saved him from a hopeless future, under what miraculous circumstances he had been able to free himself from his infernal circle. Although I was in the heart of Hinduism, I was reminded of the Gospel passage in which the apostles, encountering the blind beggar, questioned Christ about the reason for that man's cruel destiny: "Was he born blind to pay for his own sins, or those of his parents?" A sibylline phrase that all the catechists try to gloss over, since it can be interpreted as an allusion to the doctrine of reincarnation.

The boy smiled at me—or rather, through a gap in his harelip, I was afforded a glimpse of a jumble of overlapping teeth. He pointed to the basket that he had set down at my feet as if he were offering it to me as a gift. The grimy rag that covered it occasionally moved: there was something alive in there, something that every so often emitted a faint squeal. The boy tried to speak, but only a guttural croak came from his throat. Maybe he wanted to show me what the basket contained. At that moment the mission's door opened and a nun came out. "Ishan, Ishan ..." she called. Then she headed towards us. The boy who answered to the name of Ishan planted his crutches on the ground, determined not to move from there. He was about to start crying, but the nun consoled him, running her fingers through his matted hair ... I didn't understand what she was saying to him, but after a while the boy finally calmed down and started making his way towards the mission. I noticed that supported by his crutches he moved with unusual agility.

The nun turned to me. "It's a gift," she said in English, and bending over she revealed the contents of the basket. A gift? Ishan had given me a gift. I peered inside: lying on her side, on a bed of mango leaves, was a little white dog that was nursing four puppies, as tiny as mice. She must have just given birth because her fur was still sodden. The nun replaced the cloth and picked up the basket to hand it to me. Ishan, meanwhile, had stopped in the doorway of the mission to make sure I would accept his gift; there was no excuse in the world to refuse. I settled the basket on the back seat, making sure it would not tip over during the drive. A few minutes later I was already on my way back. Whereas earlier there had been caravans of oxen-drawn wagons, and whole families who were fleeing, carrying their household goods improbably loaded on bicycles, now the road seemed deserted. Darkness had suddenly fallen and there was only the beam of the car's headlights to illuminate the way. From time to time, some indistinct animal was caught blinded in the middle of the road, before leaping into the underbrush at the last possible moment. After traveling a dozen or so miles, worried that I might be going in the wrong direction, I stopped to consult the map. I spread it out on the hood of the car and with the help of a flashlight checked the route that I had taken. Before setting off again I lifted the edge of the cloth that covered the basket and saw that mama and her pups were sleeping. Who knows how much longer the little creature would have the strength to nurse them. I kept wondering where I could find them a home. India is certainly not a place with dog resorts. Perhaps I could leave them at the hotel where I was staying; being frequented mostly by Westerners, the kitchen leftovers were, for the local religion, food that could not be eaten, and therefore had to be thrown away. The second I was about to restart the engine, the deafening buzz of the tropical forest suddenly hushed, as if swept away by a surge of chilling silence. The entire world seemed to be holding its breath. Sultan Khan's words about the legend of the birds' singing masters came back to me: "Their coming will be preceded by a profound silence. It will mark the end of Kali Yuga and the beginning of a new golden age."

For an instant I dared hope that the time had come, but already reddish flashes were streaking the horizon, followed by the rumble of heavy artillery.

The conflict between the two nations left thousands dead on the battlefield and resulted in an unsatisfactory trade of sorts: some Indian territories passed over to Pakistan while, conversely, others were captured by India. The border didn't even change its trajectory, except the way a crack in the plaster can change over time. Mittha Tawana remained split into two parts. Sultan Khan died a year later, consumed by tuberculosis. His body, protected by a mound of stones, lies below the wall of the mission's garden, in the shade of the lush banyan, the sacred tree.

**ANNE MILANO APPEL** has translated works by a number of leading Italian authors for a variety of publishers in the US and UK. Her awards include the Italian Prose in Translation Award, the John Florio Prize for Italian Translation, and the Northern California Book Award for Translation. Translating professionally since 1996, she is a former library administrator, and has a doctorate in Romance Languages. Her website is: amilanoappel.com

## On the Design

As book design is an integral part of the reading experience, we would like to acknowledge the work of those who shaped the form in which the story is housed.

Tessa van der Waals (Netherlands) is responsible for the cover design, cover typography, and art direction of all World Editions books. She works in the internationally renowned tradition of Dutch Design. Her bright and powerful visual aesthetic maintains a harmony between image and typography and captures the unique atmosphere of each book. She works closely with internationally celebrated photographers, artists, and letter designers. Her work has frequently been awarded prizes for Best Dutch Book Design.

The painting on the cover is by the American artist Jeffrey Bailey (b. 1956). Bailey worked as a freelance illustrator and mural painter in the United States before settling in France, where he now paints in a variety of mediums. In his paintings, Bailey gives life to a stronger emotion through personal themes. This particular painting is from a theme called "Men-Monkeys." Other paintings in the series depict monkeys playing instruments, reading, or sitting down at dinner. A double comment, perhaps, on the nature of humankind.

The cover has been edited by lithographer Bert van der Horst of BFC Graphics (Netherlands).

Suzan Beijer (Netherlands) is responsible for the typography and careful interior book design of all World Editions titles.

The text on the inside covers and the press quotes are set in Circular, designed by Laurenz Brunner (Switzerland) and published by Swiss type foundry Lineto.

All World Editions books are set in the typeface Dolly, specifically designed for book typography. Dolly creates a warm page image perfect for an enjoyable reading experience. This typeface is designed by Underware, a European collective formed by Bas Jacobs (Netherlands), Akiem Helmling (Germany), and Sami Kortemäki (Finland). Underware are also the creators of the World Editions logo, which meets the design requirement that "a strong shape can always be drawn with a toe in the sand."